STITCHED

- Killer or Victim?

Tony Flood

STITCH UP! - Killer or Victim?

Published in the UK in June, 2020 by Tony Flood in conjunction with SW Communications.

ISBN 9798651070237

Kindle Edition | Copyright © 2020 Tony Flood

CREDITS:

**Front cover photo by Carles Rabada on Upsplash@carlesrgm
Back cover photo by Clint Patterson on Unsplash (cbpsc1)
Both covers, and the book, designed and formatted by Diny van Kleeff.**

PRAISE FOR STITCH UP!

Riveting plot and electrifying double twist. - **STUART PINK**, Showbiz Features Editor, **THE SUN**.

Stitch Up! is another superb thriller from the pen of Tony Flood. Full of suspense, with great characters and humour to ease the tension. A MUST for those who love Peter James, Jeffrey Archer and James Patterson. - **FRANCIS WAIT**, author of The Magical Pendant of Perdania under pen name FRANCIS JAYCEE.

A fast-paced read with enough twists to satisfy any thriller fan. - **TAMARA MCKINLEY**, best-selling author.

Killer or Victim? This is the question posed and answered in STITCH UP.

Tony Flood, author and newspaperman, has put his journalistic experience to good use in this thrilling, fast moving police investigation of two awful south coast murders.

Characters jump from the page. Well-written dialogue brings them alive. The carefully constructed story flows from incident to incident through a complex police examination that brings us a startling conclusion after many twists and turns.

Did the main suspect kill two young women? Guilty or Not Guilty? With red herrings galore, I could not decide until the final stunning action in a can't-put-down chronicle of lust and murder most foul. - **JOHN NEWTON**, former police officer, broadcaster and author of White Sunrise and The Assassination Diaries.

DEDICATIONS AND ACKNOWLEDGEMENTS

This book is dedicated to my wonderful wife and fellow author Heather Flood, who has given me so much help and support. It is also dedicated to the memory of my friend Alan Baker and my parents Mabel and Dennis Flood and grandparents, Win and Reg Burwash, who brought me up with so much love and kindness.

They, together with Heather and my son James, have been an inspiration to me as a writer.

I have received exceptional help with this book from a former Metropolitan Police detective, who has spent countless hours advising me on police procedures in relation to the plot.

I have also benefited greatly from edits and suggestions by John Newton, a former police officer, broadcaster and the author of White Sunrise and The Assassination Diaries.

There has been further helpful feedback and suggestions by best-selling author Tamara McKinley, actor Brian Capron and my wife Heather. They have all contributed to making STITCH UP! - Killer or Victim? a credible, fast-moving crime thriller.

I would also like to thank Diny van Kleeff for formatting both the paperback and e-versions and designing the covers. Diny, John Newton and my other former police officer friend showed enormous patience in helping me make so many changes until I thought I'd finally got things right!

OTHER BOOKS BY TONY FLOOD

TRIPLE TEASE – a spicy crime thriller endorsed by bestselling writer Peter James

*

MY LIFE WITH THE STARS - SIZZLING SECRETS SPILLED! Containing revelations and anecdotes about a host of showbiz and sports stars

*

SECRET POTION – a fantasy adventure recommended for Harry Potter fans

PART ONE

CHAPTER ONE

Friday, May 5th, 2017

Pippa Mercer was terrified as her assailant went completely berserk, waving his arms about wildly and striking her hard in the chest.

"That'll teach you a lesson, you bitch," the brute hissed.

Pippa gasped in pain. She knew she must get away and reach the sanctuary of her home across the road, but, hampered by her ankle-length blue skirt, stumbled only a few steps before the man landed a second blow.

"HELP!" she shouted. None came so she yelled at him: "Get away from me, you raving lunatic. I'd rather eat my own vomit than have sex with you."

That prompted him to go into another frenzy and he lashed out at her again. She fell to the ground, moaning in agony.

Despite covering her face with already bruised arms and hands, Pippa's lips became badly swollen and blood ran from a head wound.

She made another frantic cry: "HELP, PLEASE HELP ME!" but still nobody came to her rescue.

Her attacker stood over her, gloating.

"You pig!" she spluttered.

Two kicks from the raging man's steel-capped boot

crashed into the side of her head, bringing more blood pouring from a deep gash.

Pippa let out the screech of a dying soul before her torturous ordeal was finally over. She lay dead!

The killer was still not satisfied. He pulled up her skirt and ripped off her light blue panties which he stuffed into his pocket before fleeing.

CHAPTER TWO

Saturday, May 6th to Monday, May 8th, 2017

"Bugger!" exclaimed Detective Chief Inspector Harvey Livermore.

He was referring to the fact that nobody had witnessed the murder of Pippa Mercer despite it taking place on the opposite side of the road from the block of flats in which she had lived in Polegate, East Sussex.

But his initial disappointment turned to satisfaction by the time he had finished reading a statement given by the dead woman's next door neighbour Annu Williams.

The heavily pregnant West Indian woman had heard screams and ran as fast as she could across the road to find Pippa lifeless on a grass verge.

Mrs Williams stated this was a few minutes after 2pm by which time the killer had fled.

But she was able to provide some important evidence of an incident that occurred two nights previously when she'd heard a row taking place in Pippa's flat.

She said: "I went round to complain and could see through the front window that Pippa was being shouted at by her boyfriend Denton. He was acting in a threatening manner towards her."

Livermore's mood was later to improve even further. A

copper in the traditional restrained mould who normally avoided novelty or showiness, he was moved to shout triumphantly "YES!"

The DCI became embarrassed when this uncharacteristic outburst prompted DI Jeff Nottage, his reliable No.2 in the Major Crime Department, to come into his office without knocking.

"What's up, Gov?" he asked. "Anything the matter?"

"Nothing's the matter, Jeff. Quite the opposite. I've just received a report from the pathologist. It shows there was skin under Pippa Mercer's fingernails. This suggests, of course, that she scratched her attacker. We need to talk to her boyfriend Denton and check his DNA. He was heard rowing with Pippa two nights before her murder."

Nottage, a younger, slightly taller, leaner version of his senior officer, shared the euphoria by declaring: "If his DNA matches then it's case solved!"

When police visited Denton Kerscher, his left cheek was clearly grazed. The 31-year-old security consultant was promptly arrested on suspicion of murder before being interviewed by Livermore and Nottage in the presence of his solicitor Lloyd Knight at Eastbourne police station's custody suite.

Initial questioning by Livermore brought an admission from their suspect that he did not have an alibi because he was at home drinking at the time of the murder.

Livermore's rugged face showed no emotion when he referred to the forensic evidence. "Mr Kercher, particles of skin have been found under the victim's fingernails. This corresponds with the fact that when police visited you at your flat you had a cut on your cheek which is still visible."

The prissy Knight straightened his tie as he replied: "My client has already given an explanation for his facial wound."

Nottage was quick to respond. "Ah, yes, Mr Kerscher. At first you refused to say how you got the scratches when asked about them by my colleague Detective Sergeant O'Sullivan. Then you claimed that Miss Mercer scratched you four hours before the attack on her. You said she did so in a row at her flat that morning."

Kerscher's handsome features looked troubled. He explained: "I didn't answer at first because I thought it would look bad to admit Pippa and I had a big row earlier in the day. Now I realise that was a mistake."

Livermore could not resist raising his eyebrows dubiously. "Indeed. But who do you have to back up your claim that you went to her flat that morning? So far nobody has said they saw you arrive or leave."

Kerscher protested: "I told DS O'Sullivan that a Jehovah's Witness saw me leaving the flat. I expect one of the neighbours did, too. The busybody next door must have heard us arguing that morning."

"Unfortunately, not - only two nights previously."

"Well, one of the bible-pushers called while I was rowing with Pippa on Friday morning. The woman saw me leave."

Knight asked: "Presumably, you will continue to look for her, Chief Inspector?"

Livermore nodded. "We will, Mr. Knight." He then turned to Kerscher. "If your far-fetched story is true, why did you have a row with Miss Mercer on the day of her murder? And how did it become physical? What was it about?"

"I accused her of flirting with some other bloke who had come on to her at a party. I told Pippa what I thought of her and she didn't like it. That's when she scratched me and said we were finished."

Livermore nodded. "That gives you a motive, doesn't it?"

After closely examining further statements and evidence, Livermore charged Kerscher with murder.

Although the DCI's vast experience of more than 20 years in the Force had taught him never to take anything for granted, he felt justified in telling his team "You've done an excellent job and we should get a guilty verdict."

As Livermore expected, bail was refused, and Kerscher spent almost 12 months detained in Wormwood Scrubs.

CHAPTER THREE

Monday May 14th to Tuesday, June 12th, 2018

Denton Kerscher bitterly resented being banged up so long before his case finally came to court on Monday, May 14th, 2018. Now he had a chance to win his freedom, but felt bad about how things might turn out.

Kerscher cringed as the Prosecution barrister, a flamboyant, wily man, aptly named Oscar Fox, stressed the importance of the DNA evidence.

In his questioning of police and forensic witnesses, Fox focused on the fact that traces of the defendant's skin were found under Miss Mercer's fingernails, indicating she had scratched Kerscher in self-defence.

Detective Sergeant Michael O'Sullivan said when he questioned Kerscher the day after the murder there were scratch marks clearly visible on his left cheek.

"What did he have to say about this injury?" Fox asked.

"At first he refused to give an explanation. Eventually he claimed Miss Mercer scratched him in a row at her flat on the morning of the murder."

"Did your house-to-house calls and questioning of potential witnesses ever come up with anyone who had seen Mr Kerscher enter or leave her flat that morning?

"No, sir; I've made extensive inquiries but nobody has

supported his claim."

A distraught Kerscher's curse of "you bastard" brought him a rebuke from the judge.

Kercher felt that the longer the trial went on the worse his plight was becoming, with Fox highlighting his lack of an alibi and having an obvious motive in being ditched by the woman he loved.

'Don't panic', Kerscher told himself. *'I'll turn things round when I give evidence. I've always been able to charm women and there's six of them on the jury.'*

But the situation did not improve after he went into the witness box. His agitation masked his normal appeal despite his barrister, Hector Boyd-Samuels, asking helpful questions.

Kerscher's impassioned plea that he had deeply loved Pippa and would never inflict such a brutal attack on her seemed to impress some of the jury. But he did not see the response he wanted when he gushed: "I felt so gutted at splitting up with her in a row that morning, I was at home getting drunk out of my mind at the time of her murder."

The worried security consultant had a similar sinking feeling to that he'd once experienced when a big corporate deal collapsed. His churning stomach felt even worse as he exchanged glances with Boyd-Samuels, whose rotund face looked grim.

But towards the end of a frustrating day Kerscher noticed his barrister smile for the first time after being handed a note. Boyd-Samuels quickly spoke to the judge, who instructed that the jury be removed.

Asked to explain, Boyd-Samuels said: "M'Lud, my team have located a vital witness and I believe their evidence will have a bearing on the outcome of this case."

Kerscher's hopes rose when the judge halted proceedings to allow police time to interview the female witness and put her through an identification procedure.

Following a two-day break, a middle-aged frumpy-looking woman named Ursula Makepiece was called to give evidence. She began by muttering nervously. Kerscher willed her to speak up and was pleased to hear the silky smooth Boyd-Samuels coax her by conducting his examination in the gentlest of tones.

Kerscher listened attentively to the following questions and answers:

BOYD-SAMUELS: I believe you are a Jehovah's Witness.

URSULA MAKEPIECE: That is correct, sir.

BOYD-SAMUELS: And in your capacity as a Jehovah's Witness you visited a flat on the morning of Friday, May 5th, 2017, which you since learned belonged to a Miss Pippa Mercer,

URSULA MAKEPIECE: Yes, sir.

BOYD-SAMUELS: What time was that?

URSULA MAKEPIECE: About 10am.

BOYD-SAMUELS: Did Miss Mercer answer the door to you?

URSULA MAKEPIECE: No, sir. It was a gentleman

who came to the door.

BOYD-SAMUELS: I believe you have identified this gentleman to the police. If you see him in this courtroom can you point him out please?

Kerscher remained expressionless as she slowly lifted her right arm, pointed in his direction with a shaky hand and said "That's him."

The barrister smiled broadly and stated: "Let it be recorded that the witness is pointing at Mr Kerscher." He turned back to her and asked: "What did you say to him?

URSULA MAKEPIECE: I said I was a Jehovah's Witness and would like to talk to him about our Lord.

BOYD-SAMUELS: And how did he reply?

URSULA MAKEPIECE: He told me to go away.

BOYD-SAMUELS (leaning forward): Can you recall his exact words?

URSULA MAKEPIECE: Yes, sir. He said 'Fuck off you silly cow'.

As the courtroom erupted in laughter, Kerscher felt a mixture of embarrassment and relief. *'At least it proves she remembers me,'* he thought.

BOYD-SAMUELS: Did you see or hear Pippa Mercer?

URSULA MAKEPIECE: Yes, sir. She came to the door and said 'Sorry' to me.

BOYD-SAMUELS: What happened next?

URSULA MAKEPIECE: Mr Kerscher barged past me and left. Then Miss Mercer closed the door.

BOYD-SAMUELS: Did you notice anything about Mr

Kerscher's appearance?

URSULA MAKEPIECE: Yes, sir. He had blood seeping from a wound on his left cheek. He was dabbing it with his handkerchief.

Kerscher felt thankful that his claims had finally been confirmed. But he was on tenterhooks as Prosecution barrister Oscar Fox's summing up stressed he could have returned to kill Miss Mercer.

The worried defendant felt more encouraged to hear a beaming Boyd-Samuels tell the jury: "As intelligent people, you will have spotted the obvious flaw in the Prosecution's case concerning particles of my client's skin being found under Pippa Mercer's fingernails. We have proved this was because she had scratched his cheek that morning - four hours before the attack which killed her in the afternoon. There is, therefore, no evidence that my client murdered the poor woman. And the simple reason is HE DID NOT DO IT."

The jury took only three hours to return a unanimous verdict. "Not Guilty, m'lud", said the Foreman.

An elated Denton Kerscher pumped his fist in the air triumphantly and then broke down in tears.

PART TWO

CHAPTER FOUR

Later that day, Tuesday, June 12th, 2018

The contents of the wastepaper bin scattered on the floor as DCI Livermore angrily kicked it against the wall of his compact office at Sussex Police HQ in Lewes.

"What a bloody injustice!" he shouted aloud, cracking his knuckles.

The commotion caused Nottage to poke his head round the door. "Are you alright, Gov?"

"No, I'm not alright," raged Livermore, dropping his ample frame into his well-padded chair. "That stupid bloody jury has let a vicious murderer out on the streets again."

Nottage nodded glumly. "I'm as pissed off about it as you are, Guv. But we were..."

The phone interrupted him. Livermore answered it and had to suppress a sigh when he discovered it was Detective Chief Superintendent Frampton, his fastidious task master, known throughout the Surrey and Sussex force as 'Fussy Frampton'.

It immediately became obvious that Frampton, whose recent promotion defied logic in Livermore's eyes, wasn't calling to sympathise - but to hand out a rollicking.

"I can't tell you, Harvey, how angry I am about Kerscher being found not guilty. What annoys me most is his barrister leaving us with egg on our face by producing a witness we didn't know about."

"I'm bloody annoyed, too, sir," replied Livermore, waving to Nottage to leave the room, which he did.

"And so you should be," retorted Frampton. "Kerscher's smarmy barrister was able to drive home that this Jehovah's Witness had seen his client leaving Pippa Mercer's flat with blood running from his cheek four hours before the murder. He made the jury believe that our DNA evidence showing Kerscher's skin under her nails counted for nothing."

"Yes, sir. It's all very unfortunate. Kerscher had told DS O'Sullivan at the outset that he'd been seen at the flat by a Jehovah's Witness, but Mike was unable to trace her. He began to think Kerscher had made up the story and doubted if she existed."

Frampton fumed: "Well she certainly did. It sounds like a gigantic cockup to me. Find out from O'Sullivan why he failed to track down a key witness when the Defence team managed to do so. Her being called at the 11th hour completely wrong-footed us."

"Yes, sir. But in my opinion the jury should still have found Kerscher guilty. The fact the scratch on his cheek was inflicted in the morning doesn't prove he didn't attack Miss Mercer in the afternoon."

Unfortunately, this only made his boss more exasperated. "There was, of course, another factor which the Defence highlighted, Harvey. That was we could not find any of Kerscher's clothing or footwear contained any blood splatters which the victim's injuries would have produced."

Livermore raised his eyebrows sceptically, thinking 'so that's my fault, is it?' But he kept quiet and was left to dwell on Frampton's final words: "Either Denton Kersher disposed of his clothes and footwear very quickly and he's got away with murder - or someone else is the killer."

CHAPTER FIVE

Thursday, June 14th, 2018

Kerscher spent the next two days celebrating his court victory in his favourite pubs and going to Hastings to visit his Mother, who had always supported him. It was an emotional, tearful reunion.

On his third night of freedom he and his mates Keith Hopper and Philip - 'call me Phil' - Andrews downed pints in the Jolly Butcher at Bexhill.

"You've been greatly missed," said Hopper, who Kerscher often referred to behind his back as The Gnome because of his large, pointed ears and missing front tooth. "Have you got used to being a free man again?"

Kerscher realised that he hadn't. "Not quite, Keith. It's going to take time. Being remanded in custody for a year is something I'll never forget. When I wake up in the morning I still think I'm banged up inside the bloody prison cell. It takes me a few seconds to realise the screws aren't going to yell at me to get out of bed."

"How bad was it inside?"

"Awful, mate. You had to be on your guard the whole time in case one of the other cons took it into their head to attack you."

"Did you make a few enemies, then?" Andrews, a blunt

Scot, wanted to know.

"I kept my head down, but one of the cons, a real charmer called Chopper, resented me simply because he thought I was too good looking. He threatened to cut up my 'pretty face'."

"Blimey, so your time in the Scrubs must have been a nightmare," Hopper said sympathetically.

"True true, Keith. And the fucking place was infested with rats and cockroaches."

"Fortunately that's all behind you," reflected Andrews, with a kindly smile and patting his mate on the back.

"Not entirely. The dingy flat I've taken as a temporary measure in Hampden Park is only a slight upgrade."

The three men chuckled and took another sip from their beers.

"Have you made any plans yet, Denton?" Hopper inquired.

"No, I'm going to enjoy some quality time before I think about getting another job. Even though I was found not guilty, my old firm won't re-employ me. Let's face it, not many security companies would want to take on someone who's spent a year in the slammer."

"So what are you going to do with yourself?" asked Andrews.

"I'm going to start by enjoying my freedom. I'll take some early morning walks on the beach, away from the hustle and bustle. Sometimes I'd rather be on my own than listen to people making small talk. Present company excluded, of course, gentlemen."

Andrew's craggy face grinned. "Yeah, we provide you with intellectual stimulation, don't we?" he joked.

Hopper laughed and spilt some of his ale down his jacket. He turned swiftly to place his glass on the bar counter and, in doing so, knocked against a shapely woman who was walking past.

"I'm so sorry, luv," he spluttered, brushing drops of beer off his jacket with his nicotine-stained fingers. "Let me buy you a drink."

She looked down disdainfully at The Gnome's silly grin and said sharply: "No thank you."

Andrews, whose comb-over and puffy eyes made him little more appealing than The Gnome, also received a withering glare. But when Kerscher, an obvious upgrade in both looks and dress sense, beamed at the woman, she told him: "You, on the other hand, can buy me a drink any time."

He downed the rest of his beer and reflected: 'Thank God I've still got my good looks'.

CHAPTER SIX

Friday, June 15th, 2018

Detective Chief Superintendent Frampton carefully studied the report submitted to him by Livermore, who had questioned DS O'Sullivan at length about why he had not located Ursula Makepiece.

At 9am Frampton summoned the Irishman and immediately put him on the spot by saying: "So, O'Sullivan, how do you explain this sorry mess?"

The sergeant claimed he had been at a disadvantage because the Jehovah's Witnesses did not know which of their members - if any - had visited Pippa Mercer's flat.

He explained: "I spoke to all the members who were most likely to have carried out house-to-house calls in that area and none of them had done so. I had difficulty in locating Mrs Makepiece who was no longer working with the church and had moved away from the area after getting married. She'd left without giving the church any up-to-date details about herself - they only had an old address for her - and she'd changed her name, through marriage, from Ursula Bamber to Ursula Makepiece."

An unsympathetic Frampton did not like excuses. And he found it hard to forgive this man who he felt was mainly responsible for a shock court defeat that had left him embarrassed and his masters fuming.

He said: "Your failure to find this woman effectively lost us the case. When the Defence came up with her it completely wrong-footed us."

O'Sullivan shook his head.

"How come the Defence team found her and you didn't?"

"It could simply have come down to luck," O'Sullivan suggested.

Frampton was having none of it. "DCI Livermore told me that you took time off during the inquiry because of domestic problems you were experiencing. Did you inform him there was one Jehovah's Witness you'd been unable to trace?"

"No, sir. But I checked again with the Church and they were sure I'd spoken to all members who might have made house calls in the Polegate area at the time of the murder."

Frampton took his glasses off and stared at the wretched man for several seconds. "Well, they got it wrong - and so did you."

O'Sullivan was left to sweat for the rest of the day before being told what punishment would be meted out to him.

***

Frampton called Livermore into his office to discuss the matter.

"What do you think, Harvey? I'm tempted to report O'Sullivan to Professional Standards for neglect of duty, but I'd like your view."

Livermore took a deep breath, causing his broad shoulders to rise. He had the chance to get rid of the most unpopular member of his team, but he believed the arrogant Irishman could be a good copper despite his faults.

"O'Sullivan should obviously have informed me that he'd not fully completed his inquiries before he took time off to deal with his marriage problems. But he insists he thought he'd already spoken to all the relevant people in the Jehovah's Witnesses congregation covering the Polegate area. None of them were aware that Ursula Makepiece was still making door-to-door visits. The fact the church did not have her current address and she'd changed her name through marriage made it more difficult to trace her."

Fussy Frampton scoffed. "Well, the Defence team located her, didn't they? And her evidence swung the jury. If our barrister had known of her existence he'd have conducted the case in a very different manner. But in the circumstances I'll let O'Sullivan off with a rollicking. He's got you to thank for not being reported to Professional Standards and a possible demotion."

Livermore hoped he would not regret it.

CHAPTER SEVEN

Monday, September 3rd, 2018

Livermore heard nothing further about Kerscher until three months later when his old adversary was arrested for committing a double assault outside a Brighton nightclub in the early hours.

The DCI arranged for Nottage and PC Grace Conteh to interview him, and watched proceedings on a CCTV monitor from an adjoining room.

Kerscher sat on his side of a metal table with his solicitor, Lloyd Knight.

Nottage, having switched on a tape recorder and formally identified those present, gave a summary of the allegations.

He then turned to Kerscher. "You were caught on CCTV knocking down your new girlfriend Holly Clancey outside the Fantasy Island Nightclub and then standing over her yelling abuse. When the nightclub bouncer intervened you hit him so hard you broke his nose."

Livermore noted that Kerscher showed no sign of his usual arrogance. Instead, he slumped in his chair, head in hands, appearing to show genuine remorse.

"I don't know what came over me," he muttered.

"You were like a raging bull," said Nottage.

"That's not justified," protested Knight.

Nottage put on his glasses and scanned his notes. "Well, let me see Mr Kescher. A witness saw you kick the bouncer when he was on the ground. Then you ran off, jumped over a safety barrier as if you were an Olympic hurdler and sprinted to your car. How do you explain that?"

"I can't."

"You obviously had a row with your girlfriend and lost your temper with her," said Nottage, removing his spectacles.

Knight, who had the look of a typical upmarket solicitor in pin-striped suit, expensive shirt and distinctive tie, intervened. "That's an unfounded accusation, Detective Inspector. Your use of the word 'obviously' shows you are making an assumption - you have no direct evidence to back up that statement."

Livermore mouthed "Smart arse!" and watched Nottage try to hide a scowl. But Kerscher eased the tension with a softly-spoken admission. "I don't remember. I really don't. I've never done anything like this before."

"Are you kidding us?" snapped Nottage. "What about Pippa Mercer?"

This brought a sharp retort from Kerscher. "I was found not guilty, wasn't I?"

"Indeed you were. But you admitted having a row with Pippa at her flat on the morning of her murder that was so bad she scratched your face."

"Yes, she scratched me, but I didn't retaliate. I never

laid a finger on her."

Conteh, who strongly resembled Barbadian singer Rihanna in looks and build, spoke for the first time. "So why did she scratch you?"

"I called her a whore."

Livermore silently agreed when it became obvious that Nottage appeared to see no point in taking this line any further. Instead the DI shuffled his papers together and said: "There can be no arguments about your current caper. We not only have you on CCTV assaulting two people, but when you were found in your car you were well over the drink limit. I think it likely you'll be spending some more time in the nick, mate."

CHAPTER EIGHT

Monday, February 4th, 2019

Hector Boyd-Samuels was proud to have been given the nickname 'Mr Fixit' for repeatedly finding loopholes in the law, but the middle-aged, pompous barrister did not see himself as a miracle worker.

He had told Kerscher: "You've got yourself into a real mess this time. Even I cannot prevent you being found guilty of assault. But I might be able to keep you out of prison by showing enough mitigating circumstances, and perhaps get you off being in charge of a vehicle while unfit through drink or drugs."

"I can't go back inside," said Kerscher.

"Then we'll plead not guilty to all the charges. That will allow me to cross-examine the witnesses. I'll be asking them questions that I'm sure will solicit the answer "No" and these negative responses should minimise the mayhem your madcap antics caused."

Boyd-Samuels quickly realised that nightclub bouncer Mick Banks was an excellent prosecution witness. The man described in detail how he saw Kerscher lose his temper with girlfriend Holly Clancey as they left the club.

The muscular Banks told the court: "Mr Kerscher started shouting at her and then pushed her to the ground. I tried to hold him back, but he lashed out at me and broke my nose. When I lost balance and went down he kicked me at least twice. Then he raced off."

The bouncer's story was backed up by CCTV footage so Boyd-Samuels did not try to refute it. He knew he would have a better opportunity with Holly Clancey.

When questioned by the Prosecution barrister, a dapper little man called Basil Gaffney, she stated that Kerscher picked an argument with her, shouted abuse and pushed her, causing her to fall over. Then he yelled angrily while she was on the ground.

Boyd-Samuels observed the young woman show anxiety in the way her attractive almond-shaped eyes looked away quickly as she gave each answer.

He tried to get Holly to warm to him by flashing his most kindly smile and asked: "You've told the court that Mr Kerscher pushed you - but did he actually strike you?"

"No, sir."

"This push that Mr Kerscher gave you - did it actually cause you any injury?"

"No, sir."

"Do you remember what he said while you were on the ground?"

"No, sir."

Holly accepted that Kerscher treated her well during their four-week relationship and had behaved 'like a gentleman' earlier that night.

"Did you notice when his mood changed?" asked

Boyd-Samuels, maintaining eye-contact with the witness.

"At the end of the evening."

The smooth-talking barrister had decided to base his defence on a claim that Kerscher's last drink had been spiked. So he asked: "Would this mood change have occurred before or after he had his final drink?"

"After. He suddenly became aggressive and bad tempered."

"Would you say he changed from Dr Jekyll to Mr Hyde?"

Gaffney jumped to his feet and cried "Objection."

The magistrate peered over his spectacles and said: "Don't try to put words in the witness's mouth, Mr. Boyd-Samuels."

Unruffled, the barrister felt pleased to have made his point. He continued: "Tell me, Miss Clancey, did Mr Kerscher ever take drugs to your knowledge?"

"No, sir."

Boyd-Samuels called Kerscher as his only witness and asked him: "Do you have a clear recollection of what you did after you left the nightclub with Miss Clancey?"

"No, sir."

"Can you remember pushing her over?"

"No, sir."

"Can you remember striking Mr Banks?"

"No, sir."

Moving on, Boyd-Samuels inquired: "How did you feel the next day?"

"I was so ill I went to see my doctor. He arranged for me to have a blood test."

Boyd-Samuels turned to the magistrate and told him: "Your Worship, I offer as evidence the result of my client's blood test and examination"

Before the magistrate was able to start reading the two-page document, Boyd-Samuels added: "This shows that Mr Kerscher's blood contained a drug called Monkey Dust."

"And what the devil is that, Mr Boyd-Samuels?"

"It's man-made and also known as MDPV. It's from a family of drugs called cathinoes which include the stimulant khat. Monkey Dust can cause people to react violently and perform almost superhuman feats which explains why Mr Kerscher was able to hurdle over railings and sprint to his car like an athlete, albeit a deranged one."

This brought laughter from most of those present, with the noticeable exception of the prosecution counsel and one stone-faced figure in the gallery - a clearly unhappy Nottage.

The magistrate called for order and asked: "Is your client admitting, Mr Boyd-Samuels, that he used drugs?"

"No, sir. Our contention is that someone poured Monkey Dust into one of his drinks in the nightclub with malicious intent. In my client's further defence, I now produce another piece of evidence, in the form of a previous blood test that Mr Kerscher had as part of a medical check-up four months earlier. That test shows no trace of Monkey Dust or any other drug of any kind in his body."

With a dramatic flourish Boyd-Samuels handed the

second document to the stern-faced magistrate.

After reading and comparing both medical reports, the magistrate turned to the defendant. "If we were to accept this claim that your drink was spiked, who do you think did it?"

Boyd-Samuels listened intently as Kerscher repeated perfectly how he had briefed him to answer such a question. "I don't know for sure, your Worship. But after I was found not guilty of murdering Pippa Mercer, some of her friends and family ran a campaign against me on social media. Lots of people have a grudge against me. One of them could have slipped something into my drink while it was on the bar counter - the nightclub was so crowded I would not have noticed."

Boyd-Samuels summed up by saying in a loud, confident boom: "My client's dramatic change in behaviour is, to me, clearly explained by the very strong possibility his drink had been spiked. This is the only valid explanation as to how Monkey Dust got into his system. It caused him to act completely out of character and to dash to his car in a panic."

The barrister was delighted that his strategy resulted in Kerscher avoiding a prison sentence. He was let off with fines of £500 for common assault and assault occasioning actual bodily harm, plus a further £500 compensation to the bouncer and £300 court costs. For being in charge of a vehicle while unfit through drink or drugs he was given a £1,000 fine and a 12-month driving disqualification.

Boyd-Samuels smiled as Kerscher showered him with praise. The smile got even bigger as Nottage walked past them, clearly seething.

CHAPTER NINE

Monday, February 4th, 2019

Kerscher had another night of celebration with his mates Andrews and Hopper - this time in the Golden Swan, Eastbourne, which he was able to walk to following his driving ban.

They got talking to a salesman who helped them form a four-man team in the pub quiz.

"What's your name, mate?" asked Hopper.

"Charlie Kaye," said their new smartly-dressed friend. "And you guys?"

Kerscher, himself wearing fashionable polo jersey and designer jeans, completed the introductions. "I'm Denton Kerscher, this is Keith Hopper and he's Philip Andrews."

"Call me Phil," insisted Andrews.

Kerscher got in a round of drinks and when he returned was surprised to hear Kaye taking a keen interest in Hopper, asking him: "Do you have an allotment by any chance, Keith?"

"Yes, how to you know?" Hopper replied cautiously.

"You must be the good Samaritan my wife's been telling me about. You've given vegetables to her and other members of the church, haven't you? And you mended the church gate, too. My wife and her friend Mavis have been singing your praises."

Hopper beamed.

"Quite the hero," said Kerscher, patting his friend on the back.

The quiz proved to be more difficult than they anticipated, particularly The Gnome.

Kerscher rebuked him after he gave three incorrect answers, saying: "You've gone from hero to zero, Keith. A broken clock could do better than you - at least it's right twice a day!"

This brought a glare from The Gnome until Kerscher assured him: "It's only a bit of banter, Keith." He gave his friend another pat on the back.

Their team, which they had named The Rascals, enjoyed a change of fortune in the second half of the quiz, with Charlie Kaye excelling.

But the final question - 'which famous British murderer of women in the 19th century was never arrested?' - brought some puzzled looks.

Seeing that Hopper was clearly flummoxed, Kerscher quipped: "Why are you pulling that face, Keith? Are you concentrating or have you got constipation?"

"Probably both," joked Andrews.

When the laughter subsided, Kaye said: "The Ripper."

"What?" asked Kerscher.

"The Ripper was never arrested. I thought you'd know the answer to a question about murder, mate."

Kerscher scowled at him.

CHAPTER TEN

Tuesday, February 12th, 2019

Vinnie Rowlands was a towering 6ft 5in giant who fellow villains called 'The Elephant Man' - but never to his ugly face!

Rowlands wasn't severely deformed like Joseph Merrick, about whom the film The Elephant Man was made. It was just that his ears and nose were enormous.

And, like an elephant, Rowlands never forgot, particularly when someone upset him.

He had spent 10 years banged up in jail and every day of that time he vowed to get his revenge on the man who'd put him there - Detective Chief Inspector Harvey Livermore.

Rowlands had killed a rival drug dealer and claimed it was self-defence. At worst, he'd expected to go down for manslaughter. But Livermore helped get him convicted of murder by telling the court he believed Rowlands had the intention to kill or cause grievous bodily harm.

The policeman's damning evidence cost him everything, including his marriage, a luxury home near London as well as a villa in Spain and two top of the range cars - now he had virtually nothing.

Since coming out of prison two weeks ago he'd been living in a grotty bedsit above a boarded-up shop in

Eastbourne, plotting to get his own back.

Rowlands found out from one of his underworld contacts where Livermore and his wife lived and was determined to torment them. But he would bide his time.

The chain-smoking thug cursed after finding he'd run out of cigarettes and thought: *'My life's shit. I'm going to make that bloody copper's life shit, too.'*

CHAPTER ELEVEN

Friday, February 15th, 2019

Fewer thefts, assaults and domestic disturbances than usual were showing up on the police computer logging reported incidents in East Sussex.

This gave Livermore the chance to catch up with a mountain of paperwork in his cramped office, a much smaller room than he had enjoyed prior to the move from Sussex House, Brighton, to the police HQ in Lewis.

He was doing just that when Nottage knocked on his door and entered.

"I've got some news you'll find very interesting, Guv."

Livermore could not suppress a smile as he surveyed his colleague's new closely cut hair.

"Seems the barber took a dislike to you, Jeff," he said.

"Yeah, the idiot cut it too short," admitted Nottage, taking a seat. "At least it's given the team something to laugh about this morning."

"Nice of you to go to that trouble to cheer them up, Jeff. Anyway, what have you got to tell me?"

"Yesterday a 19-year-old young lady called Barbie Dickinson claimed she'd been raped in her flat in Hampden Park."

Livermore nodded. "Yes. I caught sight of it. I believe it

was actually called in by her boyfriend, wasn't it?"

"That's right. She had phoned the boyfriend, Gavin Johnson, telling him she'd been assaulted. He raced round to her flat to find her in a state of distress, with part of her clothing torn. So he rang 999.

"Miss Dickinson was interviewed at our Sexual Assault Referral Centre in Crawley and was reluctant to give all the details, which, of course, isn't unusual when assault victims are traumatized.

"But the Sexual Offences Liaison Officer Pauline James coaxed her to reveal what happened and Miss Dickinson has now provided a full account. Pauline has just informed me that a recording of their interview can be accessed on our database. I think it will be of particular interest to you."

"OK, let's look at it, then," Livermore said. He gestured to Nottage to take a seat and found the digital recording on his computer.

It showed a plain-clothed Pauline James talking to an agitated Barbie Dickinson, wearing a track suit as a change of clothing, while sitting on uncomfortable chairs in an interview room.

"When am I going to get my clothes back?" asked the victim, biting her lower lip and showing further signs of nerves by tapping her fingers on the table which separated them.

"As I believe my colleague explained to you, Barbie, we need to examine them for possible traces of DNA from the man who you claim attacked you. Now, I appreciate how difficult this must be for you, but please tell me what happened."

"I've already said that this bloke grabbed my breast so hard he bruised it. Your doctor has seen how swollen it is. And you've got my blouse which was ripped."

"Yes, but you need to explain the assault in detail."

Barbie just stared at the officer blankly.

Pauline tried another tack. "Your boyfriend told us you knew your attacker."

Again Barbie did not answer.

"How was he known to you, Barbie?"

Finally, the attractive peroxide blonde relented. "He's a new resident who's moved into a flat on the floor above mine. He called to collect a parcel the postman left with me while he was out."

"And did you let him in?"

"He came into my hallway because that was where I'd left the parcel."

"Did you have a conversation with him?"

"He did the talking. He said how much he appreciated me taking in the parcel. Then he asked what perfume I used and told me it smelt great. But I felt uneasy because the sod wouldn't take his eyes off my boobs and then made some remark about me being a real 'Barbie Doll' with a lovely figure.

"I asked him to stop staring at my breasts. The creep claimed it was my fault for wearing a low-cut top and said he'd love to stroke them. I told him not to be so bloody cheeky. But he took no notice and copped a feel."

She took a deep breath and lowered her head. "He squeezed my right tit so hard it hurt like mad. I pushed him away but he pulled down my bra and fondled one of my nipples."

When Barbie stopped talking, Pauline encouraged: "You're doing well. Which nipple did he fondle?"

"It must have been the left one. If he'd touched the right one again I'd have freaked out completely."

"At what stage did your blouse become torn?"

Barbie paused for thought. "That was when he stroked my nipple. I tried to knock his hand away and my top got ripped."

"What happened next?"

"He took out his cock and rubbed it against me."

Barbie started to sob and was given a handkerchief to wipe away the tears from her reddened cheeks.

"Did he lift your skirt or remove any more of your clothing."

"No."

"Are you sure?"

"Yes, that was it."

"Do you know if he ejaculated?"

"I wasn't watching! But I put a stop to his antics by kneeing him in the balls. I then pushed him out of my flat and bolted the door."

An impatient Livermore halted the recording. "Why should this sexual assault be of particular interest to us in the Major Crime Team, Jeff?"

Nottage returned his boss's frown with a smile.

"Because the guy who took 'greeting your new neighbour' to a whole new level was Denton Kerscher."

"What!" exclaimed Livermore, raising his eyebrows in surprise.

"Yes, he'd moved into the flat above Barbie only a week earlier."

"So this confirms what a perverted bastard Kerscher is," Livermore reflected. "But he didn't actually rape her."

"No, Guv. She and her boyfriend were wrong to call it rape. But it's clearly sexual assault. Hopefully, there'll be traces of semen on her clothing or other evidence. But busty Barbie's testimony and the injury to her breast should be enough for Kerscher to be charged and convicted."

Livermore beamed. "Yes, perhaps his luck is starting to run out."

**

Kerscher, having been arrested for sexual assault and indecent exposure, was released pending the CPS deciding whether he should be charged.

When Livermore next discussed the case with Nottage they expressed contrasting views.

Nottage lamented: "There's no supportive evidence - no semen or anything. And nobody witnessed or heard the assault."

Livermore grinned at his colleague's change of attitude. "Don't be so pessimistic, Jeff. Last time we spoke you were confident of Kerscher being charged and convicted. That could still happen. The pictures of Miss Dickinson's bruised and swollen right breast, plus the torn low-cut top she had almost been wearing should be enough for the CPS to charge him."

This brought a more positive response from Nottage. "Yeah, you're right, Gov. And the CPS should also be influenced by the fact Barbie phoned her boyfriend immediately."

Livermore agreed. "Yes, the boyfriend's statement backs up how distressed she was by her ordeal and the painful injury to her breast. I think Mr Kerscher will find himself back in court.

"Of course, he insists Miss Dickinson is a fantasist and a liar. We will just have to hope she proves to be a more convincing witness than him."

CHAPTER TWELVE

Wednesday, March 13th, 2019

The night of Wednesday, March 13th, 2019 proved to be unlucky for Holly Clancey.

She'd been driving home after visiting her friend Mandy when her Ford Focus spluttered to an abrupt halt.

The fact she was only a quarter of a mile from her apartment did not improve Holly's mood because it was lashing down with rain, almost 11pm and she had forgotten to bring her mobile phone with her.

'You've only got yourself to blame,' she thought.

The car had cut out briefly the previous week but she hadn't taken it to a garage, and now the bloody thing wouldn't go at all.

Holly tried to restart the engine four times without any success. She put up the bonnet but there was no sign of any steam or anything out of place.

"Damn," she muttered as the rain began to ruin her newly permed hair style. The long strands soon became a tangled mess.

She did not hear the approaching footsteps and was unaware of the man behind her.

He tapped her on the shoulder which made her jump, but she relaxed when his familiar voice said: "Can I be of any help to a damsel in distress?"

Holly turned abruptly and exclaimed, with relief: "Oh, it's you."

"Yes, it's me," he confirmed, smiling. "What's the matter - your car's packed up, has it?"

Without waiting for her to reply, he added: "You get back inside and try starting it again while I take a look."

After two abortive attempts, her new companion removed his gloves and checked a few things under the bonnet. "It could be the battery or something more serious. Perhaps the fuel pump has gone."

"So there's nothing we can do?" Holly sighed.

"No. I suggest I walk you home and you call out the AA in the morning."

As it was no longer raining, Holly agreed and, after locking the car up, they walked along the four streets to her apartment.

He made her laugh when he joked: "Your new 'drowned rat' hairstyle suits you."

She thought the least she could do was invite him in for a coffee. He accepted and followed her example by removing his wet shoes in the hall leading to her front door.

It did not occur to Holly until they were in her lounge that her guest might assume there would be more on offer than just a cup of coffee. *'Well, if he does, he'll be bitterly disappointed'.*

CHAPTER THIRTEEN

Wednesday, March 13th and Thursday, March 14th, 2019

Livermore was in a much happier state of mind.

Kerscher had been charged with sexually assaulting Barbie Dickinson, with a reasonable prospect of him being convicted, and the DCI was finally getting through the pile of paperwork on his desk.

He had mentioned this to his wife Evelyne and, at her insistence, booked three days' leave to celebrate her 51st birthday. They were due to depart on Friday for a two-night stay at a hotel in Rye.

Livermore admitted the short break would do him good. His recent heavy work load had caught up with him so he went to bed early Wednesday night and was sleeping soundly until the persistent ring tone of his mobile woke him from his slumbers shortly before 1am.

"Yes," he bellowed into the phone next to his bedside.

"Sorry to disturb you in the middle of the night, sir," said the familiar voice of his trusty inspector Nottage. "But there's been a murder."

"Hold on a minute, Jeff." Livermore jumped out of bed, whispered "sorry" to his disturbed wife, and took the cordless phone on to the landing to prevent fully waking her.

"Okay. Give me the details."

"A young woman has been killed in her apartment in Eastbourne. I'm there now."

"Alright, Jeff. Give me the address and I'll join you as soon as possible."

Nottage provided the details and added: "There's one other thing you need to know, Guv. She's been identified as Holly Clancey, the girlfriend who Denton Kerscher assaulted outside a nightclub."

Livermore caught his breath. "So he could be our killer."

***

Upon arriving at Holly Clancey's second floor apartment Livermore donned white protective clothing and shoe covers to prevent contaminating the scene with his own DNA or transferring materials from other locations.

The apartment was full of Crime Scene Investigators - formerly known as Scenes of Crime Officers - led by Neville Kilby, and forensic pathologist Stefan Gilchrist.

Livermore did not wish to get in the way of the white-suited officers who were busy dusting surfaces for prints and gathering evidence in clear plastic bags to be sealed airtight. So he began by calling Nottage over to bring him up to speed.

"Miss Clancey was struck on the head with a blunt object," the DI reported. "The killer was almost certainly known to his victim because she had made two cups of coffee. These were presumably knocked over by her falling during the attack. Her scream and the commotion alerted the man in the apartment immediately below who then heard someone running from the building. This occurred around 11.30pm.

"The neighbour, a pensioner called Joe Cowdrey, came up to Miss Clancey's apartment to see if she was alright. The door was wide open so he looked inside and found her dead. Mr Cowdrey is still being questioned by O'Sullivan and Dimbleby."

Livermore entered the lounge and viewed Holly Clancey's battered head and crumpled body, lying on the floor in a mass of blood. He quickly surveyed the contemporary designed apartment before speaking to Kilby and Gilchrist in the hall, but they could tell him very little.

A glum Gilchrist said: "It seems Miss Clancey was taken by surprise. She was hit on the head at least twice by a blunt, relatively flat object, probably the marble ashtray which was left lying on the floor near her body. It's covered in blood.

"There are no initial signs of the killer sexually assaulting her, but it would appear that after delivering the fatal blows he removed her panties. They're missing so he presumably took them with him."

"Perhaps she wasn't wearing any," suggested Livermore.

"She WAS," insisted the pathologist. "I've spotted marks on her body where the waistband of the panties would have cut into her. That was likely to have been caused by the killer ripping them off."

Livermore nodded. "So there's a chance of us discovering the killer's DNA and his fingerprints."

Gilchrist did not share his optimism. "Possibly, as long as the old chap from the apartment downstairs did not contaminate them. But there's no apparent traces of the killer's skin under his victim's fingernails - or, at least, none are visible to the naked eye. He probably caught her completely off guard - she appears to have used her left arm to deflect the blows but didn't get a chance to put up a fight."

"And what was the likely time of death?"

"There's no sign of rigor mortis and the eyelids are still flaccid so I'd say not much longer than an hour before I started to inspect the body. I may have more to tell you after the post-mortem."

"Anything to add, Nev?"

"Not much at this stage. There's no indication of forced entry, and Miss Clancey had apparently been happy to make coffee for her visitor so she hardly expected him to attack her."

Livermore shook his head. "It doesn't make much sense, does it?"

CHAPTER FOURTEEN

Thursday, March 14th, 2019

Nottage was feeling far from his best when he left the crime scene with Conteh to pay Kerscher a visit.

He'd been up shortly after 5am to take his parents to the airport for their holiday to Greece and lack of sleep was beginning to have an effect as he and Conteh arrived at 2.45am at Kerscher's new second floor flat on the outskirts of Eastbourne.

Despite ringing the bell repeatedly they got no answer.

"Perhaps he's still not returned home," said Nottage.

Conteh nodded. "Possibly - or maybe he's been drinking and is so spaced out he can't hear us. What do you think we should do?"

Nottage, unshaven and in a sweat-stained, crumpled shirt, was feeling uncomfortable and tired. He replied: "Let's go home, get some sleep and come back at 8am. I'll arrange for one of the uniforms to stay out here until then in case Kerscher emerges in the meantime."

When Nottage and Conteh returned at eight, PC Brian Hudson reported that there had been no sign of Kerscher.

They tried the bell again and after the fourth ring were buzzed in. Kerscher's flat was the third one on the second floor and he was waiting at the door, bleary-eyed, unsteady on his feet and fumbling to fasten the cord of his dressing gown.

"What's so fucking important that you need to wake me up?" he demanded, slurring his words as he reluctantly allowed them into his messy lounge.

"This is very important, Mr Kerscher," Nottage assured him, side-stepping a half empty bottle of whisky that had been left on the imitation wood panelled floor.

"OK, what is it, then?"

Nottage ignored the question and asked one of his own. "When did you last see Holly Clancey?"

"Months ago. Why?"

Again the stern-faced Nottage did not provide an answer, but came up with another question: "Where were you last night...and who were you with?"

"Why, what's it got to do with you?"

"I'm asking because Holly Clancey was found dead last night."

"What?" Kerscher's demeanour changed and the hostility was gone. "How did it happen?

"She was murdered. Where were you between 10pm and midnight?"

"Oh, no. You're not going to try to fit me up for that as well."

"So where were you?" repeated Nottage.

"Excuse me," mumbled Kerscher. "My mouth is so dry I can hardly speak." He went into his kitchen, poured himself a glass of water and downed most of it before returning to face them.

Nottage reminded him: "I was asking where you were?"

"Drinking in the Golden Swan. Then I came back here."

"If you were here why didn't you answer the bell when we rang it at 2.45 this morning?" asked Nottage.

"Because I was in bed dead to the world. I'd had several beers in the Golden Swan and then sat here watching TV and drinking whisky." He pointed to the bottle on the floor.

"What time did you leave the Golden Swan?"

I was there until around closing time and plenty of people must have seen me."

"But that's not far from Miss Clancey's apartment," Conteh pointed out. "You could have driven there within a few minutes."

"If you'd done your homework properly you'd know I'm banned," Kerscher snapped. "I haven't driven for over a month."

Conteh refused to back down. "OK, you could have walked to her apartment in 10 minutes."

"Well, I didn't," insisted Kerscher, pulling his dressing gown around him. "I was no longer seeing Holly - we'd broken up ages ago. You've no reason to suggest I had anything to do with this. I haven't done..."

Nottage cut short the man's protests. "Your assault on Miss Clancey outside the Fantasy Island nightclub, followed by the allegation concerning Miss Dickinson, doesn't put you in a good light, does it? Add to that the fact you were within ten minutes of Miss Clancey's apartment last night when she was killed..."

An irate Kerscher interrupted him. "Like I've repeatedly told your colleagues, that stupid woman Barbie invented the whole story about me trying it on with her. And the incident outside the nightclub with Holly and the bouncer was due to someone spiking my drink. It's crazy that you should think I had anything to do with her murder."

"Is it?" asked Conteh softly. "Two women who went out with you have both ended up killed. There's one obvious link to them - and it's you."

Kerscher turned and hurried to his kitchen where he threw up in the sink.

When the pasty-faced man returned, Nottage upset him even more by informing him: "I am arresting you on suspicion of murder. You do not have to say anything, but it may harm your defence if you do not mention when questioned something you later rely on in court. Anything you do say may be given in evidence".

Kerscher eye-balled Nottage. "I've only got one thing to say: this is a fucking stitch up!"

CHAPTER FIFTEEN

Thursday, March 14th, 2019

When Livermore had returned home in the early hours of Thursday morning he'd been greeted with the sound of a harsh Scottish voice demanding: "Where the devil have you been, Harvey?"

Evelyne was coming down the stairs in her dressing gown and had gone without the beauty sleep she clearly needed.

"Sorry luv," he said soothingly. "There's been a murder."

"Don't tell me that it's going to delay us leaving for our trip to Rye tomorrow," she snapped.

"I'm afraid it will cause our hotel stay to be postponed, dear."

"WHAT! We haven't had a break for months and now you're cancelling it."

"Not cancelling it - just postponing. It's very unfortunate, but you know I have to drop everything when a murder occurs. A young woman has been killed and she must be my priority."

"That sums up our life together, doesn't it, Harvey? You pay more attention to a dead woman than you do to me."

It crossed Harvey's mind that looking at the poor

lifeless victim had been less distasteful than facing his raging wife now.

Evelyne carried on her tirade as she stormed to her bedroom and emerged again at the top of the stairs with her small suitcase. "This was obviously a waste of money!" she shouted, taking from the case a brand-new Ann Summers nighty which she hurled at him.

"It's always the same, Harvey. Your job comes first and I come last - even to a corpse."

"That's not fair, Evelyne."

"Isn't it? If I ran about the house naked banging a drum you wouldn't notice me."

Livermore was anxious to remove this image from his mind. He did so by replacing it with thoughts of the dictionary definition he had once read for the name 'Evelyne' - a creative, beautiful, intelligent, talented girl who can make everyone smile. Sadly, the woman he'd fallen in love with more than twenty years ago no longer matched that description.

He tried again to console her. "I'll make it up to you, I promise. Let's have a cup of tea, shall we?"

But Evelyne refused to be placated. Their row and the atmosphere it created made it impossible for him to snatch more than a couple of hours' sleep before returning to work.

CHAPTER SIXTEEN

Thursday, March 14th, 2019

Livermore felt exhausted at 9.30am as he tried to switch from henpecked husband to assertive leader of a murder investigation team. Starting the briefing meeting by using a hand to hide a yawn didn't help.

He looked around the Major Incident suite, packed with members of the Major Crimes unit plus profiler Ralph Vickers and Jennifer Duggan from the Public Relations Department.

Most of those seated at workstations or on chairs around the grey-carpeted room were fully focused on what Livermore had to say. But Nottage and Conteh, like their boss, were trying to suppress yawns.

Livermore kicked off the proceedings for the first meeting of Operation Flamingo by pointing at a white board on which he had written the names of the latest murder victim and her relatives, the possible time of her death and the location of the crime scene.

"These are the basic facts," the DCI began. "We know that Holly Clancey was killed by two or more blows to the head by a blunt, flat object - probably a marble ashtray found on the floor near her body with blood all over it. But I've checked with forensics this morning and there don't appear to be any clear fingerprints on the ashtray so the killer could have been wearing gloves."

"That suggests it was a planned murder," said Dimbleby.

"Perhaps, but not necessarily, Chris. The killer may have worn gloves simply because it was such a cold, wet night."

"Wouldn't he have taken them off if it was unplanned?" the veteran officer suggested.

"It depends upon how long he had been in the apartment," his chief replied.

Nottage stood up to make a point. "Surely, he didn't drink the coffee he was given with his gloves on. There should be a set of his prints on his cup."

"We live in hope, Jeff. But it could be that the killer didn't bother with the coffee - perhaps he just launched an unexpected attack on Miss Clancey."

"What about footprints, Gov?" asked Conteh.

"Forensics may come up with something there, but we mustn't be too hopeful. Mr Cowdrey, the pensioner from the apartment below who discovered the body, appears to have contaminated some of the crime scene by walking over it. He even touched the body to check if Miss Clancey was dead."

There was a brief silence during which Livermore added on the white board next to him the name 'Pippa Mercer'.

"As with the murder of Pippa Mercer, for which Denton Kerscher was tried and acquitted, the killer apparently flew into a rage. And once again there was no sexual assault as such, but it again appears he ripped off his victims' panties after she was dead.

"So, although Pippa was killed by multiple kicks and Holly by blows from a blunt instrument, it could have been the same man."

This was a cue for O'Sullivan to vent his anger. "And that man is Denton Kerscher," he stormed.

Livermore held up a hand to stop the rant continuing. Then he announced: "In view of Kerscher's history, the fact he was Miss Clancey's ex-boyfriend and he was within ten minutes of the crime scene we've arrested him on suspicion of murder. We're currently searching his flat."

He then asked Nottage to bring everyone up to date with the visits he and Conteh had made to Kerscher.

Nottage came to stand at the front of the room and explained that Kerscher had not answered his door at 2.45am. "When we returned at 8am he told us he'd been spaced out after drinking in the Golden Swan and then downing a couple of large whiskies at home. He certainly seemed to be the worse for wear. He was slurring some of his words and looked unsteady on his feet. Kerscher insisted he had nothing to do with Holly Clancey's murder. He says they were no longer going out together."

"So what time did he leave the Golden Swan?" asked Dimbleby.

"He reckons he was there until 'around closing time'. We'll be talking to other customers today. If they confirm he was in the pub up to 11.30 then his alibi could stand up."

O'Sullivan again called out from the back of the room. "People often get confused about times so that's not going to be conclusive, is it? Kerscher got away with murdering Pippa Mercer partly due to my cock-up, but surely there'll be reliable DNA or CCTV evidence this time."

Livermore smiled ruefully. "There's no CCTV cameras in operation near Miss Clancey's apartment, but hopefully the forensic team can tie Kerscher to the crime scene. Our search of his flat may find her knickers, and his clothes could have traces of blood on them."

O'Sullivan was not convinced: "He might already have dumped the shoes and clothes he was wearing last night - just as he must have done in the murder of Pippa Mercer."

"You may be right," Livermore concurred. "A thorough search of the area will be made. But we must look at other possible suspects as well."

He glanced across at analyst Helen Yates and asked: "Helen, can you check on assaults on women of a similar nature that have been committed in recent years, particularly where the offender has taken any items of his victims' underwear as a trophy. Widen the search by looking at other forces' case histories as well as ours."

"Yes, sir," said the toothy twenty-something woman.

"I've already uncovered one new suspect," piped up Chris Dimbleby.

"And who's that, Chris?" Livermore inquired.

"Miss Clancey's boss. She worked for Fabio

Camaggio's fashion house as one of his designers."

There were a few sniggers because it was known that Dimbleby was not a fan of designer clothes and had a dislike of Italian men since his first wife ran off with one of them.

"So what makes him a suspect in your book, 'Dim'?" O'Sullivan asked sarcastically. "The fact you can't afford to buy his clothes or simply because he's Italian?"

"No, Mike. The fact he has a history of touching up some of his staff and is known to have exposed himself to one of his models and then asked her to perform a sex act."

This brought a mixture of gasps of surprise and giggles at O'Sullivan's discomfort.

"Sorry, Chris," mumbled O'Sullivan, forced to grudgingly respect a point made by the usual butt of his humour.

Livermore felt it necessary to add: "Let's cut out the put-downs, Mike. And no more calling Chris 'Dim', eh? OK, Chris. Tell us more."

"Well, Camaggio was taken to an industrial tribunal by two female employees for sexual harassment and apparently settled out of court with the model. I'll be making further inquiries to see if he tried it on with Miss Clancey."

Before Livermore could reply his mobile phone rang. He took the call and what he was told by the caller clearly surprised him.

The DCI clicked off his phone and told his team: "That was the pathologist Stefan Gilchrist. He's just finished the post-mortem and it reveals that Holly Clancey was pregnant."

***

The only additional information Livermore could give was that the murdered woman had been pregnant just over two months.

"So Kerscher could have been the father," said O'Sullivan. "I..."

Conteh cut in. "He says they'd broken up."

"We can't take that man's word for anything," scoffed O'Sullivan, his voice rising in anger. "But even if that's true, they may still have been in a relationship two months ago. He could have been the father."

Conteh was quick to point out: "If they were carrying on at that time it was while Kerscher was waiting to go to court for assaulting Holly. That would be breaking his bail conditions."

Livermore brought the exchange of views to an end by saying: "We can easily find out if Kerscher is the Daddy. We'll see whether his DNA matches that from the foetus. If that shows it was him then he'll have some more questions to answer. Did he know? - and was it a bone of contention between him and Holly?

"Meanwhile, I'd like Mike and Chris to pay a visit to Mr Camaggio."

CHAPTER SEVENTEEN

Thursday, March 14th, 2019

Fabio Camaggio was now 69 years old, with thinning silver hair, bushy eyebrows and a pot belly. Yet despite the ageing process and the fact he was just five foot seven inches tall in platform heels, he still believed women were attracted to his looks rather than his money.

Even two expensive sexual harassment cases - and three very costly divorces - had not dented his massive ego.

He was now leaning back on the white leather sofa in his luxury penthouse admiring the gorgeous young lady sitting on a chair opposite him.

"So Cindy, you want to be a model," he said, flicking through the pages of her portfolio. "The pictures of you are impressive, but you've very little experience. Show me why I should give you a job in my fashion house."

He smirked as Cindy crossed one shapely leg over the other, causing her short blue skirt to rise and reveal her bronze thighs.

"What did you have in mind, Mr Camaggio? Would you like me to model some swim wear for you?"

"I've got a better idea," he said. "Come and stand in front of me."

As Cindy, a 19-year-old brunette with long, flowing

hair, sauntered over to him, he asked: "What are you wearing under your skirt and blouse?"

"White undies and stockings and suspenders, as you requested, Mr Camaggio."

"Show me."

Cindy's pouting lips turned into a cheeky smile as she slowly lifted her skirt until her suspenders were visible.

"Take off your skirt, dear," he commanded.

She obliged, revealing her white panties.

"Lovely," he said. "Would you also be interested in nude modelling for magazines catering for the male market?"

"Maybe."

Camaggio walked across to his desk and sat behind it, causing Cindy to turn and face him. He produced a couple of men's magazines which he held up for her to see.

"I have a share in these. To consider you for them I need to be sure you've got special sex appeal, Cindy. Do you know how I can tell?"

"No, Mr Camaggio."

He glanced down at the bulge in his trousers and smirked; then stared at the naive young woman in her state of undress.

"Take down your panties."

She blushed.

The ageing Italian liked this girl. She had a quality few women in modelling still possessed - a touch of innocence!

"Is there a problem?" he asked, unzipping his trousers

while hidden by the large desk top.

"No, Mr Camaggio."

Cindy wavered before slowly tugging down her skimpy panties. He breathed heavily and admired the shaven cleft between her legs.

"Au natural!" he exclaimed, relishing her discomfort. "Ah, no. I am mistaken. You have a very tiny heart-shaped tuft of hair. It is magnifico."

The young woman corrected him: "It's not a heart, Mr Camaggio. It is a dove."

Actually having a conversation with Cindy about her pubic hairs added to his arousal. The blatant lothario gasped as he used his out-of-sight left hand to pleasure himself. Within seconds he ejaculated into his silk underpants.

"Magnifico!" he said again. "You have passed the test."

The shameless fashion supremo watched the embarrassed job applicant get dressed, zipped up his trousers, and told her: "I'll be in touch."

CHAPTER EIGHTEEN

Thursday, March 14th, 2019

Two hours later Fabio Camaggio, his short frame still encased in a silk grey suit, showed a different side of himself while being interviewed in his spacious office by O'Sullivan and Dimbleby.

Dimbleby took an instant dislike to the man - in his eyes an older, richer version of the suave Italian who had run off with his wife.

O'Sullivan asked: "Mr Camaggio, what sort of relationship did you have with Holly Clancey?"

"Are you suggesting I behaved improperly towards one of my employees, Sergeant?"

"Well, did you behave improperly with Miss Clancey?"

Their host raised his prominent eyebrows in disapproval and said: "Have you any idea how insulting it is for me, a serious businessman and upright citizen, to be asked such a thing. The answer is 'No, I did not'."

Dimbleby coughed to register his disbelief. This caused the immaculately attired fashion tycoon to give his new, poorly dressed, adversary a disdainful glare. The policeman, determined not to be undermined, wrong-footed Camaggio by asking him: "Are you familiar with Shakespeare? If I may slightly misquote a line from Hamlet: 'Me thinks thou doth protest too much'. You were taken to an industrial tribunal by two female employees for sexual harassment, weren't you?"

"They were telling lies," Camaggio retorted. "After being dismissed, they concocted those ridiculous stories. They were very convincing and the industrial tribunal awarded them costs, but what they accused me of was utter bullshit."

"And the model Evette who accused you of exposing yourself to her and asking her to perform a sex act?"

"More fabrication."

"So why did you make her an out of court settlement of £250,000 and get her to sign a non-disclosure agreement?" Dimbleby persisted.

"To prevent her spreading foul and completely untrue accusations, of course. You obviously don't appreciate that rich men like me are easy targets for unscrupulous women who want to make easy money."

Dimbleby exchanged skeptical glances with his fellow officer who asked: "Did you have cause to regard Miss Clancey as one of those sort of women?"

"No. I didn't know her very well. She was a junior member of our design team so she wasn't directly responsible to me."

"Come on!" insisted Dimbleby with a smirk. "Holly was a beautiful woman - not unlike the model to whom you paid £250,000."

Camaggio, as large on arrogance was he was small in

stature, glared at him. "My only contact with Miss Clancey was on a purely professional basis. There was no relationship between us. I only saw her as a good employee."

When O'Sullivan and Dimbleby questioned some of Camaggio's staff they endorsed that Holly Clancey was a highly respected, likeable colleague. But they were reluctant to point the finger at their boss as a sexual predator.

The two officers found one notable exception, however. Disgruntled designer Gabriel De la Cour, serving his notice prior to starting a new job with another fashion house, was more forthcoming.

Speaking hurriedly in a French accent, he said: "Yes, Monsieur Camaggio does like the ladies and he often flirts with them. But I have rarely seen it go any further than him making the odd suggestive remark."

"How much further did you see it go?" asked O'Sullivan.

"He patted a couple of the girls on the backside," said De la Cour."

"Girls?"

"I mean ladies, Monsieur."

"How old were they?"

The foppish designer made an extravagant hand gesture. "Oh, they ranged from about 18 to 40, I suppose."

"Anything else?" pressed O'Sullivan, looking sternly at the Frenchman.

"Well, at the office Christmas party Monsieur

Camaggio dressed up as Santa and got some of the girls - ladies - to sit on his lap. None of them objected, but the randy old sod asked them what they would like him to give them."

This brought another smirk from Dimbleby. "What about the industrial tribunals and the settlement Camaggio made to the model called Evette?"

"What went on behind closed doors I can't say. But he didn't sexually harass or blatantly grope anyone in front of me. All I witnessed was him being a bit over familiar. He loves to flirt."

"And did he 'flirt' with Holly Clancey?" pressed O'Sullivan.

De la Cour nodded. "I overheard him sweet talking her a couple of times. She just laughed it off and told him she had a boyfriend."

"That would be Denton Kerscher," Dimbleby suggested.

The designer shook his head. "She dumped Monsieur Kerscher some time ago. Holly then started going out with a young stud called Rodney something or other. He worked as an estate agent for Barnett and Lythe."

"Do you know anything more about Rodney?" Dimbleby queried.

De la Cour pushed back his long, wavy hair and smiled. "Not much. Holly hadn't been going out with him long. But he must have been very keen on her. He twice sent flowers to her at the office."

Dimbleby made a note in his book: 'Rodney - new

suspect. Camaggio told us a pack of lies'.

The cynical copper muttered to himself: "I'd just love to put this slimy big shot behind bars."

CHAPTER NINETEEN

Thursday, March 14th, 2019

Livermore asked Conteh to assist him in conducting an interview with Kerscher that did not take place until 1pm. This was because his solicitor Lloyd Knight claimed his client needed additional time to fully recover from a hangover and fatigue.

The DCI tried to keep sarcasm out of his voice as he began by asking: "Are you now fit to answer our questions, Mr Kerscher?"

After receiving a curt 'yes' in response, Livermore said: "You claim you were drinking at the Golden Swan last night, Mr Kerscher. What time did you leave?"

"I already told this young lady and your colleague when they got me out of bed this morning that I was in the pub until around closing time."

"What time would that be?"

"I can't be certain because I'd had a skinful and then drunk a couple of large whiskies when I got home. I lost track of time, but it was well after 11. The landlord and customers can confirm it."

"We'll be talking to them," Livermore assured him. "You say you did not go to see Miss Clancey."

"No I didn't. I couldn't be in two places at the same

time, could I?"

Conteh responded. "I pointed out to you that the Golden Swan is not far from Miss Clancey's apartment - it wouldn't have taken you long to walk there."

"And I told you I didn't. I had no reason to do so because we were no longer seeing each other."

Kerscher glared at Conteh across the hard metal table at which they were seated in the stark interview room.

Livermore looked at the notes in front of him. "You said you had not seen Miss Clancey for months. How long ago exactly?"

"We'd stopped going out after I was charged with assaulting her outside the Fantasy Island nightclub last September."

"So you were no longer in a relationship?"

"No."

Kerscher's answer caused Livermore to rephrase his next question. "Does it surprise you that the post-mortem has shown Holly was two months pregnant?"

Kerscher looked shaken. "I didn't know," he said. "She didn't tell me anything about being pregnant."

"Let me ask you again: did you and Holly continue or resume a relationship after you were charged with assaulting her?"

"Yes," came a sheepish reply.

"Despite the fact your bail conditions made it clear you were not supposed to interfere with witnesses. That's a criminal offence, Mr Kerscher."

Knight interceded. "My client doesn't have to comment on that," he said, flicking a speck of dust off his pin-stripe suit.

"He doesn't need to!" Livermore fired back. "In my book, he interfered with a witness in every sense by having sex with her."

Kerscher protested. "It wasn't like that. I didn't set out to influence Holly about what to say at the trial - she simply told the truth. But she accepted that I only attacked her because someone spiked my drink. There was still a bond and a big physical attraction between us. It wasn't fair to expect us not to see each other for the five months leading up to the trial."

"So perhaps you could tell us the truth this time. When did you finally break up?"

"Less than a month ago. Holly being forced to give evidence against me in court put a big strain on both of us. Then came the false accusation against me by that idiot Barbie Dickinson - that finally put paid to any hope Holly and I had of making a 'go' of it."

"When did you last see Holly?"

"That would be the end of February, just after I was arrested for supposedly touching up Barbie Dickinson. It was the final straw for Holly."

Livermore brought the subject back to the pregnancy. "I suggest it was after you had broken up that Holly told you she was expecting your baby."

"That's not true."

"Perhaps she asked you to provide financial support for the baby. You lost your temper and attacked her."

"Rubbish!" snapped Kerscher. "I loved Holly. But it doesn't matter what I say, does it? You're not going to believe me, are you? You bastards have already ruined my life. Nobody will employ me now and no woman is going to want to go out with me."

The interview was interrupted by Michael O'Sullivan entering the room. Livermore could tell by the excitement in the officer's face that there was some vital new information.

***

In the corridor, Livermore asked: "What is it, Mike?"

"You're not going to believe this, Gov. Neville Kirby's crime scene boys have found a very angry message on Holly Clancey's answerphone. Let me play it to you."

He ran the recording which was short and sharp: "This is Denton. I'm furious with you, Holly, for making a wisecrack on social media about the size of my dick. If you do anything like that again I'll bloody kill you."

When Livermore and Conteh resumed the interview with Kerscher, the DCI played the answerphone message.

He noted that his red-faced suspect appeared even more rattled than he had been by the news that Holly was pregnant. He asked him: "Why did you make this threat to kill Holly?"

"You don't have to say anything," Knight told his client.

But Kerscher responded. "I was furious with Holly for ridiculing me on Instagram. When I phoned she wasn't in, so I left the message telling her to cut out the insults. But what I said was just an empty threat. It's an expression people use. I obviously didn't mean I'd literally kill her. It's bang out of order you arresting me."

Livermore did not accept the explanation. He said: "I must now advise you that you are also under arrest for making 'threats to kill' in contravention of Section 16 of the Offences Against The Person Act 1861."

After being cautioned and asked if he had anything to say, a furious Kerscher snapped: "I simply tried to stop Holly insulting me on social media. This is a sick joke."

Knight put a restraining hand on his client's arm before adding: "Mr Kerscher has a point. You've come up with this spurious 'threat to kill' because you have no evidence against him for the murder of Miss Clancey."

Livermore cracked his knuckles in disapproval. "It's far from spurious, Mr Knight. He's admitted leaving a threat to kill on Miss Clancey's answerphone. Therefore, we're entitled to arrest him for that, which, incidentally, carries a maximum term of imprisonment of 10 years.

"As for the murder, so far your client is the only person we've discovered who is linked to both Miss Clancey and to the previous murder victim Pippa Mercer."

Knight protested. "My client was found not guilty of killing Pippa Mercer. This link you refer to is simply a very unfortunate coincidence."

Livermore raised his eyebrows. "If that's the case Mr Kerscher must be one of the unluckiest suspects I've ever come across."

***

While O'Sullivan was making some telephone inquiries, Dimbleby told Livermore and Conteh about the outcome of their findings at Fabio Camaggio's offices.

"Well done, Chris," said the DCI. "So we can't discount Camaggio or this new boyfriend Rodney as potential suspects. But Kerscher remains top of our list."

"Are we able to place him at the scene of the crime, Guv?" asked Dimbleby.

"Yes, but not necessarily on the day Holly Clancey was killed. Fingerprints may show that Kerscher had been in her apartment, but he can claim that was because he was there on previous occasions. I'm taking nothing for granted - we all know what happened after relying on DNA following the murder of Pippa Mercer. We don't want to be left with egg on our faces again."

Dimbleby concurred. "Ideally, we need some additional evidence."

Livermore told him about the threat Kerscher had left on Miss Clancey's answerphone.

"So what does he say about that?" asked Dimbleby.

"He claims he'd just found out Holly had ridiculed him

on social media. I've looked up what she said and it's a belter. She'd posted a picture of him on Instagram with some of the lyrics from the song 'Master of the House' in the musical Les Miserables."

"And which lyrics would they be, Gov?" Dimbleby wanted to know.

Livermore looked at his notes before answering. "Hilarious but quite insulting ones, Chris. I've written them down. Ah, here they are:

Master of the house? Isn't worth my spit!

Comforter, philosopher and lifelong shit!

Cunning little brain, regular Voltaire

Thinks he's quite a lover but there's not much there!"

When they had stopped laughing, Dimbleby made a serious point: "No wonder Kerscher was furious. But making a threat to kill her and actually doing it are two very different things."

"I accept that," Livermore conceded. "But this shows he had a motive."

Conteh concurred. "Yes, Holly's Instagram post and Kerscher's response clearly proves there was bad feeling between them following their split."

Livermore nodded. "OK. Let's see whether or not the Golden Swan customers back up Kerscher's alibi. But at this stage we can't prove he went to Miss Clancey's apartment last night. We've come up with no CCTV evidence - nothing so far.

"Let's spread our net to thoroughly investigate other

likely suspects. We need to check out Camaggio and Miss Clancey's latest boyfriend Rodney and look for anyone else who could have had a motive to kill her."

CHAPTER TWENTY

Thursday, March 14th, 2019

Nottage took PC Brian Hudson with him to visit Howard and Shirley Clancey in their detached bungalow on the Bird's Estate, Langney.

The couple were devastated and Shirley burst into tears as soon as they were asked about their daughter.

Nottage directed his questions to Howard who was holding up better and told him what he wanted to know.

"We last saw Holly at the weekend," said the tall, gaunt man, his voice cracking with emotion. "We went into Eastbourne with her on Saturday and visited her apartment on Sunday evening for a small dinner party."

Nottage encouraged Howard to continue by giving him a kindly smile. "Was anyone else at the dinner party?"

"Yes, Shirley's sister Joan."

"Did Holly say anything about who she might be seeing later in the week?"

"She told us she was planning to go out with her new boyfriend Rodney."

"Rodney?"

"Yes, Rodney Plowright. He's an estate agent with Barnett and Lythe."

"What did Holly say about Mr Plowright?"

"She told us he was a very nice bloke and we would have to meet him."

"Presumably Holly was no longer seeing Denton Kerscher."

Shirley recovered sufficiently to provide an answer. "No, thank goodness. Do you think he had anything to do with her death?"

Nottage repeated his kindly smile. "I'm sorry, but I can't comment on that. Are you aware when your daughter last saw Mr Kerscher?

"Quite a while ago, I think," Shirley answered, letting out another sob. "I just can't believe that our beloved daughter is dead. We had such a lovely weekend together." She took a tissue from a box on a side table and wiped her eyes.

"Did Holly bump into anyone she knew when you were out with her on Saturday?"

"Yes," Shirley replied. "We saw her friend Mandy on the pier. I think they arranged to meet again this week."

Howard confirmed: "That's right. We actually had a picture taken with Holly and Mandy by a photographer on the pier He persuaded me to have copies mounted for Holly and ourselves and put into silver frames."

PC Hudson looked across to the sideboard and said: "That's it, is it?"

This brought an emotional response from Shirley Clancey. She pointed to the picture and murmured: "We never dreamed that would be the last photo we'd ever have with our lovely daughter. We thought it was a bit expensive but it's priceless now."

***

Nottage phoned estate agents Barnett and Lythe to be told that Rodney Plowright was on leave.

After obtaining Plowright's address, the DI and PC Hudson went to his flat and found the smartly dressed young man preparing to go out.

Plowright had the look of a rugby player, complete with crooked nose, but when Nottage spoke about the death of Holly Clancey his face turned ghostly white.

"I can't believe Holly's dead," Plowright said. "I just can't believe it." He flopped so hard into one of his contemporary chairs that it creaked loudly.

Nottage, finding it hard to express a great amount of sympathy to someone who could turn out to be the killer, asked his questions.

"Had you known Holly for long?"

"Only a few weeks."

"How many weeks?"

"Five at the most."

"So how many times did you go on dates with her?"

The well-built man was no longer engaging. Instead, he began to shake his head and muttered "This is awful, just awful."

"Mr Plowright, I asked how many dates you had?"

"We went out twice and spent one evening together at her apartment."

"Were you with her yesterday?"

"No. I tried to phone her last night but her mobile just went to answerphone."

"And where were you last night, sir?"

"I was here doing some work and watching TV."

"Can anyone confirm that? Did you see anyone?"

"No, I..."

He was interrupted by the doorbell ringing and a male voice calling out: "Are you ready, Hot Rod?"

"Look, I have to go, Inspector. That's my friend Toby calling to pick me up. Perhaps we could continue this chat some other time." The man took out a business card from his wallet and added: "Here's my contact details."

Nottage accepted the card but told him: "This is a murder investigation, Mr Plowright, so 'some other time' will have to be tomorrow morning. We'll also need to get your fingerprints for elimination purposes and your DNA. Please come to the police station at 9am prompt."

Plowright nodded.

Nottage decided he'd wait until they spoke tomorrow to find out if Plowright had known Holly was pregnant.

CHAPTER TWENTY-ONE

Thursday, March 14th, 2019

Vinnie Rowlands was resisting the temptation to take his revenge on Livermore too soon.

'If I do it within the first few weeks of being released from the Scrubs then even the dim-witted rozzers might work out it's me,' he thought as he sat chain-smoking in his dingy flat.

But his determination to make the copper pay was so strong it had become an obsession and Rowlands knew he wouldn't be able to contain himself much longer.

The thug had already done his reconnaissance work by checking out Livermore's home in Saltdean and what times he and his wife were usually at the property.

A plan to set it on fire with the pair of them inside was very appealing. But he told himself: 'That can come later. I'll start by tormenting them and making their lives hell.'

His first objective was to make sure he wasn't spotted and, if he was, that nobody would be able to identify him. So he began walking with a stoop to give the impression of being much less than 6ft 5in tall.

CHAPTER TWENTY-TWO

Thursday, March 14th, 2019

The next meeting of the Major Crime Team's Operation Flamingo at 6.30pm brought some interesting updates.

Livermore announced that Kerscher had admitted being the father of Holly Clancey's unborn child.

"When Grace and I spoke to him this afternoon he owned up to breaking his bail conditions while awaiting trial for assaulting Miss Clancey by continuing to see her and having sex with her. He claims she had not told him she was expecting, so it wasn't a bone of contention between them.

"What I want to know is whether his alibi for last night holds up - what have you found out Chris?"

Dimbleby reported that the customers he and DC Valerie Jones had questioned at the Golden Swan could not remember Kerscher being there at closing time. Nobody was sure when he left, with one exception - his mate Keith Hopper.

The DS informed his colleagues: "Hopper is adamant that he was talking to Kerscher until after 11.30pm. Hopper says he went outside to have a smoke and got chatting to Kerscher for quite a time before they went home."

"So he reckons they were talking outside the pub in the

rain?" questioned O'Sullivan.

"There's a covered area just outside the pub. Hopper says he went there to smoke and Kerscher joined him."

Livermore rubbed his jutting, bristly chin and sighed. "If that's true, and Miss Clancey's neighbour is right about hearing someone running from her apartment at that time, then Kerscher could not have killed her."

"One of them must be wrong," yelled O'Sullivan from the back of the room where he was sitting on the side of a desk. He spluttered as he almost choked on the sweet he was chewing.

"It's a choker, isn't it?" joked Dimbleby, evoking laughs from his colleagues.

A red-faced O'Sullivan finally recovered to put his scepticism into words by blurting out: "Hopper is probably trying to help his mate by giving him an alibi, or the neighbour may have got his time wrong."

Livermore decided to humour the excitable sergeant. "You may have a valid point, Mike, but if both Hopper and the neighbour won't budge then it would be very hard to prove Kerscher was at the crime scene. Hopefully, our house-to-house inquiries may produce something."

O'Sullivan was not placated. "It's obvious to me that Kerscher carried out the threat he made on Miss Clancey's answerphone to kill her."

Dimbleby protested. "That message may have been just an expression he used in the heat of the moment."

"Yes," Livermore acknowledged. "He claims he didn't

mean it. But the assaults Kerscher committed previously on Miss Clancey and a bouncer outside the Fantasy Island Nightclub would suggest this was a serious threat."

O'Sullivan again called out from the back of the room. "Too right. The threat shows just how much he was pissed off with her. But banging him up for a few years on making a threat to kill isn't enough. We want to put him away for murder, don't we?"

Livermore nodded but pointed out: "Unfortunately, we've got very little in the way of evidence yet. The post-mortem on Miss Clancey and the forensics don't offer us anything so far - nothing under her nails, no clear fingerprints on the possible murder weapon and no DNA. We're still waiting for the analysis of any footprints, but there's apparently none in the apartment - only outside in the hall."

"Surely, there must be footprints inside?" asked Dimbleby

"Unfortunately not, Chris. We must assume that the killer took his shoes off before he entered her lounge. People are often asked to do so when they visit someone who takes a pride in their home."

O'Sullivan chipped in: "You wouldn't know about that, Chris! Your place is probably a tip. But this is no laughing matter. This bloody man Kerscher seems to have a charmed life."

Conteh held up her hand and spoke without waiting to be acknowledged. "The allegations by Barbie Dickinson should help to build up our murder case against him, shouldn't they?"

Livermore nodded once more. "Possibly, but we need to find some hard evidence. Meanwhile, what updates have we got about other suspects?"

"Well," said Nottage, "Miss Clancey's parents told PC Hudson and I about her latest boyfriend Rodney Plowright so we paid him a visit. He seemed devastated on learning of her death, though he'd only been on three dates with her. Anyway, he says he did not see her yesterday. He tried to telephone her mobile, but it went to answerphone."

"What do you make of him?" asked Livermore.

"As an estate agent, you'd expect him to have the gift of the gab, but he seemed in a complete state of shock - perhaps too much so. He was hard to read. The thing is he hasn't got an alibi - he claimed he was at home alone at the time of her death. He's coming in tomorrow morning to resume our interview and provide fingerprints and DNA."

Livermore took a deep breath before responding. "We need to do some digging on Mr Plowright."

CHAPTER TWENTY-THREE

Friday, March 15th, 2019

Livermore joined Nottage in questioning Rodney Plowright, who seemed more composed than the previous day despite the bleakness of the interview room.

The estate agent answered their questions fully but claimed he did not know Holly was pregnant.

"You had no idea?" asked Livermore.

"None at all. How far gone was she?"

"Two months."

Plowright looked stunned. "So it can't be mine." He shook his head.

Nottage, getting a nod from his senior officer, took over the questioning. "I thought you and Miss Clancey were having a meaningful relationship."

"We were."

"Yet you're claiming she did not tell you she was pregnant by a previous boyfriend"

"She didn't."

Livermore decided to use the 'good cop, bad cop' routine, with him being the 'bad guy' on this occasion. "I suggest Holly did inform you she was expecting. And when you found out it was by another man you lost your rag."

Plowright's self-control vanished. "That never

happened," he raged, rising to his feet in anger.

"Please remain seated," Livermore instructed as the large man towered over them.

"I'm sorry," said Plowright, calming down. "But I did not even see Holly on the day she was killed." He sat back in his chair.

"That's some temper you've got," Livermore observed. "Did you lose it with Miss Clancey?"

"No way. You've got this all wrong. Things couldn't have been better between Holly and me."

Livermore inhaled deeply before replying: "And yet you claim she didn't tell you she was pregnant."

***

Following the interview, Nottage received a call on his mobile from his wife Kim, telling him that she'd received a request for them both to see the headmistress of their 13-year-old daughter Niki's school as soon as possible.

"What's it about?" he asked.

"Apparently, Niki got into a fight with another girl who came off worse and needed medical treatment. The headmistress wants us to see her today, so can you make it, Jeff?"

Nottage sighed. "She couldn't have chosen a much worse time, love. As you know, I'm in the middle of a murder case. Could you handle this on your own?"

He heard Kim return his sigh with one of her own. "I

suppose I'll have to. But if Niki's landed herself in big trouble and they want to expel her then you'll have to get involved."

***

Livermore decided to delay interviewing Kerscher again until later that day by which time he hoped to have received a detailed forensics report. Meanwhile, he called the next meeting of Operation Flamingo at 10.45am and asked profiler Ralph Vickers to attend.

The DCI started by telling the team of the interview with Plowright, and then called upon Grace Conteh, who was able to report where Holly Clancey had spent Wednesday evening.

"She was at her friend Mandy Jefferson's flat, Gov. I've spoken to Mandy and she reckons Holly was with her until after 10.30pm. Holly had been in good spirits and didn't seem to have any worries. Denton Kerscher was no longer a part of her life, and she was looking forward to another date with Rodney Plowright."

Livermore was puzzled. "If Holly was so happy why did she insult Kerscher on Instagram?"

"That was an old post, Gov - it just took a while for Kerscher to become aware of it. Holly and her friends had been comparing notes about men's shortcomings on Facebook and it seems she decided to have a pop at Kerscher who she'd recently written off. Holly told Mandy she really liked Rodney Plowright and meant to phone him that evening but forgot to bring her mobile with her."

Livermore nodded. "That all checks out. Automatic Number Plate Recognition cameras showed Holly driving her Ford Focus towards her home at 10.57pm. We located the car left four streets away from where she lived. The engine was dead so we can assume she had a breakdown and probably walked the rest of the way home.

"Three sets of footprints in the hall leading to Holly's apartment have been analysed. Because it was raining on Wednesday night, they were muddy and quite distinctive. One of them matches Holly's shoes and there are two larger sets which appear to be those of men. We're in the process of checking the shoes of Kerscher, Camaggio and Plowright.

"As I said previously, there are no footprints in Miss Clancey's actual apartment so it's likely that she and her visitor both took their shoes off. It would seem that she welcomed him in and things were quite amicable when she made some coffee. Then something happened or was said to cause him to attack her.

"He picked up a marble ashtray and struck her with such brute force that it probably did sufficient brain damage to kill her before he landed a second blow. The initial forensics report showed that traces of the victim's blood and hair were on the ashtray, but no fingerprints."

Conteh put up her hand.

"Yes, Grace?"

"Do we believe the same man killed Pippa Mercer?

And what were his motives?"

Livermore acknowledged: "Those are key points. Let me hand over to our profiler Ralph Vickers." He looked across to the back of the room at a tall, thin man with a comb-over.

Vickers stood up, puffed out his chest and spoke softly but clearly.

"The evidence is not sufficient to tell us whether we can definitely assume it was the same man. The attacks were, of course, different in that the first saw the victim virtually kicked to death, and the second victim was struck two or three times with a blunt object.

"But there are similarities. In both cases the attacks were carried out in a frenzy, and, although the victims were not sexually assaulted, the fact that the killer took their knickers as a possible trophy suggests both murders were sexually motivated.

"I am therefore of the opinion that they were carried out by the same man. My experience as a behavioral analyst, suggests he is a deeply disturbed individual."

Vickers paused for breath long enough for Conteh to ask: "Are we looking for a sociopath or psychopath?"

"Not necessarily. I don't think the killer is without emotion or guilt, but I can't be sure."

The profiler was about to lower his thin frame into his chair, when Livermore pressed him further. "Can you say why he may have gone into a frenzy?"

Vickers straightened up and, after a brief pause, replied.

"That's the 64,000 dollar question, Chief Inspector. The two murdered women might both have rejected him or said something to antagonise him. This could have been the trigger which caused him to attack them, probably in a blind rage."

Nottage interrupted. "Then it wasn't premeditated?"

Vickers coughed, cleared his throat and continued: "I don't think so. The women may both have given their killer some news he didn't want to hear. Or perhaps what they said was seen by him as an insult and hit on his weak spot. It may have reminded him how he'd been rejected or humiliated in his formative years. That would explain why he reacted so violently."

CHAPTER TWENTY-FOUR

Friday, March 15th, 2019

Jennifer Duggan, a former journalist in her late twenties, was proving a valuable asset to Sussex Police's Public Relations team.

With the head of the Press Office Stella Rudd on holiday, Jennifer's latest task was to help devise a media strategy regarding the murder of Holly Clancey.

She must find a way to warn women there was a killer in the area, but do so in a way that did not panic them.

The Press release she had issued now prompted a telephone call from reporter Gerald Truelove, a freelance whose stories appeared in various papers, including the local Argus where they were once colleagues.

"Hello, Jennifer," he greeted in his superior tone of voice that had always grated on her. "I just wanted to clarify something."

"What can I do to help you, Gerald?" she asked cautiously.

"Well, you don't say in your Press release if the police believe Holly Clancey was killed by the same man who murdered Pippa Mercer a year ago."

Jennifer, a pleasant, unassuming young woman who wore little make-up, cleared her throat and gave herself some thinking time. "We don't know at this stage," she said.

"So the police are looking for two men," the reporter shot back.

"I didn't say that."

"Well, it's either one man or two men - which is it?"

"At this stage we can't be certain," she insisted.

"That means the female populations of Brighton and Eastbourne could be in danger from two murderers," he surmised.

"I can only say it's a possibility that we're looking for two killers, but neither can we rule out it being the same man."

"And do the police believe that man to be Denton Kerscher?"

Jennifer was caught off guard, but quickly composed herself and gave the standard reply: "No comment."

"That's not a denial, is it, then?" Truelove gloated.

"I said 'no comment'," she repeated.

"Look Jennifer, I know that Kerscher's been arrested and questioned about this second murder so he's obviously a suspect."

"No comment," she said for the third time.

"And off the record?"

"I don't know any more than you apparently do, Gerald."

The tenacious journalist was not satisfied. "It would appear that Kerscher, who was acquitted of the first murder, is now the chief suspect for the second murder. And please don't keep fobbing me off with 'no comment'."

She felt trapped and conceded: "Mr. Kerscher is a person of interest who is helping us with our inquiries."

"I think I've got my story," Truelove told her. "Thanks for your help, Jennifer. Why don't we have a drink sometime?"

"I don't think so, Gerald," she said, remembering how he had always goaded her when they worked together. "We've never been bosom pals, have we?"

"But we had a good working relationship," he claimed.

"You thought so, did you? Do you really think I enjoyed being called 'Blondie'?"

"Sorry about that, but I'm a changed man, darling."

The 'darling' was the final straw.

"You mean you're not quite such an overbearing, pompous, wind-up merchant as you used to be."

"That's not funny, Blondie."

"It's not meant to be funny, Gerald. They say a leopard can't change its spots - and neither can a male chauvinist pig."

Too late, Jennifer realised her mistake. Truelove's story would almost certainly not be to her liking - nor that of DCI Livermore!

CHAPTER TWENTY-FIVE

Friday, March 15th, 2019

Livermore was informed that many of Kerscher's fingerprints had been found in Holly Clancey's apartment.

He shared the news with Nottage. "There's several in the bedroom and lounge, including on individual items. But they could have been made when he was in the apartment a month or more earlier."

Nottage asked: "Would those items include a silver frame containing a picture taken on the pier of Holly with her mother and father and her friend Mandy?"

Livermore checked the list he'd been given. "They do as a matter of fact. Why do you ask?"

He looked up to see Nottage smiling broadly. The DI told him: "When I went to see Miss Clancey's parents they said they'd gone shopping with her on Saturday to prepare for a small dinner party she gave on Sunday. While they were in Eastbourne they had their picture taken together on the pier and purchased two silver frames for copies of it, giving one to Holly. So if Kerscher's prints are on that frame it means he's been to Holly's apartment since Saturday."

Livermore's mood instantly lifted. "And that rubbishes his claim he had not seen Holly for a month. Well done, Jeff.

I think we've got him! This is irrefutable evidence."

***

Nottage looked at his mobile and found he'd missed two calls from his wife.

He rang her and asked: "What's up, love? Has Niki been expelled?"

"Fortunately, not. I pointed out that Niki insists the other girl, Rita Fry, started the fight between them by pulling her hair. But the headmistress is concerned how badly Rita was hurt. Niki accepts that she went too far. She deeply regrets what she did and, as a result, she's being let off with two weeks' suspension."

"That's a relief!" exclaimed Nottage. "You've done well, Kim. Perhaps you should become a barrister."

"I don't regard it as a victory," his wife told him. "Rita Fry hasn't been suspended. She's got away with just one period of detention."

"How come?"

"Apparently her black eye has developed into a real shiner and the headmistress wanted to placate her mother. I'm furious because Niki had her hair pulled and was punched in the stomach."

Nottage opted for black humour. "There's a lesson to be learned there - aim for the body, not the face!"

***

Livermore opted to have Nottage assist him with the next questioning of Kerscher who had a new moan.

"That cell you've put me in is fucking terrible," he said. "The mattress is paper thin and the bed's rock hard."

"Sorry it's not to your liking," replied Nottage. "Were you expecting four-star accommodation?"

Livermore adopted a less confrontational approach. "We have a concern about your fingerprints in Holly Clancey's apartment, Mr Kerscher."

Kerscher's solicitor Lloyd Knight, again dressed immaculately in a pin-striped suit, jumped in. "My client has already told you he visited Miss Clancey several times before they broke up."

Livermore cut the officious man short. "Please let your client answer, Mr Knight." He looked across at Kerscher. "You told us that you had not seen Holly for a month, but some of your prints in her apartment are more recent. I'm referring in particular to those on a silver frame containing a picture of Holly with her parents on the pier."

Knight persisted. "What possibly makes you think these prints are more recent?"

"Because the picture and the frame were only purchased on Saturday," replied Livermore.

Kerscher's mouth fell open.

Livermore felt now was the ideal time to use the same tactic he had employed against Plowright. "I put it to you that you were in Holly's apartment on Wednesday night. That you attacked and killed her."

"No!" snapped Kerscher. "I had nothing to do with her murder. I wasn't there."

Livermore said calmly: "Your prints would appear to prove otherwise."

"OK," Kerscher blurted out. "I was there earlier in the week - on Monday."

"But you told us you had not seen Miss Clancey since February."

"That's true. She wasn't there when I went to her apartment on Monday."

"How did you get in?"

"I had keys to the front door of her block and her apartment door. I never got around to giving them back to her."

Livermore glanced at Nottage in disbelief. He then focused on Kerscher, waiting for him to explain.

"I went to collect a spare pair of designer jeans and expensive sneakers I'd left in Holly's apartment," he finally volunteered.

"So why did you suddenly feel you needed them?" asked Nottage.

"Holly had threatened to throw them out. I've still got her email on my laptop telling me that."

"Why didn't you tell us about this earlier?"

"I thought it would look bad for me if I told you I had keys and had let myself into Holly's apartment. You'd jump to the conclusion that I could have gone there on Wednesday, which is exactly what you're doing now."

Livermore shook his head. "That's because it's the most likely explanation. It's far more plausible than this latest story of yours about going there without permission on Monday. Why didn't you simply arrange with Miss Clancey to collect your stuff from her when she was at home?"

"Because I'd already left that angry message on her answerphone after discovering she'd ridiculed me on Instagram."

"Did you come across any of Holly's neighbours when you allegedly entered her apartment block on Monday?"

"No."

Nottage took up the questioning. "If you only went to pick up your jeans and sneakers why did you touch a picture of Holly and her parents?"

"I hadn't seen it before - it just caught my eye so I had a look at it."

"There are many more of your prints in the apartment. If they were old ones, as you've claimed, it's odd that they were not wiped away when Miss Clancey was cleaning."

Kerscher grinned. "Holly wasn't one for doing housework. Cleaning and polishing weren't her thing."

Knight pompously added: "I'll be interested to discover how many of these fingerprints would actually be admissible in court. As you know, the rules state that at least 16 points of identification on each print have to be shown."

Livermore decided to move on. "You say, Mr Kerscher, that you were in the Golden Swan pub on the night of the murder, but most of the customers we've spoken to cannot remember you being there at closing time."

Knight interjected. "I understand that one customer, Keith Hopper, has already told you he was talking to my client OUTSIDE the pub until at least 11.30pm."

Nottage made another of his sarcastic responses. "Ah, yes, your friend Mr Hopper."

Further questioning failed to produce any admissions, and there was an angry outburst by Kerscher, who insisted he was being 'fitted up' by the police.

This prompted Knight to claim, in a calmer manner: "I have to protest that you have led the media to believe my client is the chief suspect for a murder he did not commit."

Outside the interview room, Livermore and Nottage exchanged rueful looks.

"It takes the biscuit, doesn't it, Jeff," Livermore said with a shake of his head. "Kerscher insists he didn't kill Pippa Mercer or Holly Clancey or assault Barbie Dickinson. The fact he's linked to all three women is just an unfortunate coincidence, according to him and his solicitor."

CHAPTER TWENTY-SIX

Friday, March 15th, 2019

Livermore gave Fussy Frampton an update so that paperwork could be forwarded to the CPS to decide if Kerscher should be charged.

He then held a meeting of his team and told them: "We're still trying to build a case against Kerscher, but we must not make the mistake of focusing so much on him that we ignore other potential candidates."

This brought a few murmurs until Livermore held up his hand and asked: "What can you tell me about the other suspects?"

Conteh spoke first, revealing that she'd paid a visit to estate agents Barnett and Lythe and spoken to a charming young lady named Rhian Jennings.

The young DC said: "Rhian was the only staff member in the office at the time and that proved very useful because I was able to get a woman's view on Rodney Plowright. Rhian thought he'd fallen for Holly in a big way and she was pleased for him, especially as it meant he paid less attention to her."

"How to you mean?" asked Livermore.

"Rhian told me she's had to put up with sexist remarks from her male colleagues and Plowright's been one of the biggest offenders. He was very tactile and often made comments about her appearance. It was nothing blatant, as in the case with Fabio Camaggio, but if she wore a short skirt or plunging neckline, she'd catch Plowright staring at her."

Dimbleby was scathing. "He sounds a bit of a slimeball to me" and received support from an unexpected quarter.

O'Sullivan piped up: "Chris may be right. I've been checking out the local strip clubs and porn shops. None of them can recall having either Kerscher or Camaggio as customers, but I discovered that Plowright regularly hires dirty videos."

Livermore raised a note of caution. "That information could prove useful, but porn videos and websites are watched by millions of men - and women. Obviously, that doesn't mean they're potential murderers."

O'Sullivan was not deterred. "Our Mr Plowright has been watching the really hard stuff. Look, nobody wants us to nail Kerscher for this murder more than me, but Plowright could be a genuine suspect."

Nottage agreed. "You're right, Mike. I've got my doubts about him. And we can't rule out the odious Camaggio, either."

Livermore concurred. "Let's find if Plowright and Camaggio might have known the first murdered woman Pippa Mercer."

He was about to give the task to O'Sullivan but the experience with the Jehovah's Witness put a doubt in his mind. So he opted for someone he considered to be more thorough and asked Nottage to take care of it.

The DCI then turned to crime analyst Helen Yates. "Have you got anything, Helen?"

The middle-aged redhead stood up to answer. "As you requested, Guv, I've checked on previous violent attacks on women, particularly those in which they had their underwear taken. I've discovered that five men fit this profile. Three are currently in prison and another is in hospital following an operation, but the fifth, a 23-year-old Pakistani called Jawad Zirak, should be of interest to us.

"He's been convicted of two sex attacks in the past five years and took his victims' knickers as a trophy on the second occasion."

Livermore needed someone to check out Jawad Zirak and felt O'Sullivan would be better suited to this more specific assignment.

He looked at the Irishman and said: "From a galaxy of talent at my disposal, I'm selecting you, Mike, to do a complete check on this guy and speak to the women he assaulted. Take one of our young detective constables with you."

He then added the name 'Jawad Zirak' to his white board.

CHAPTER TWENTY-SEVEN

Friday, March 15th, 2019

Livermore was called into Fussy Frampton's office to discuss what should be done about Denton Kerscher.

"It's decision time," Frampton said bluntly. "We can't detain Kerscher much longer without charging him. As you know, his 36 hours in custody will soon be up."

Livermore was taken by surprise. "I thought you'd want to ask a magistrate to grant us a further extension."

"It might not be a good idea if we're unable to charge him with murder. I gather we're not in a position to do so."

"No, not for murder, but we can charge him with making a threat to kill," Livermore replied firmly.

Frampton frowned. "That's up to the CPS, Harvey. Unless you can give me any further information to pass on to them, they may decide it's not advisable at this stage, partly because we're still investigating other murder suspects."

Livermore persisted. "Surely we have enough evidence concerning his threat for you to recommend to the CPS that Kerscher be changed, sir."

"I prefer to leave it up to them," Frampton said. "If it emerges that he is our man then it might be better to use evidence of him threatening to kill Miss Clancey as part of a murder case, rather than proceed with it separately."

'Hogwash!' thought a seething Livermore, taking his frustration out on his bruised knuckles. *'This is political. Frampton and the CPS won't want to be left with egg on their faces again as they were when Kerscher was found not guilty of murdering Pippa Mercer'.* But he confined himself to replying: "So you're saying we might have to let him go, sir."

Frampton peered over his glasses and confirmed: "That's exactly what I'm saying. The CPS will be advising us of their decision soon."

Seeing Livermore's glum reaction, his senior officer added: "Don't worry, Harvey. If Kerscher made the attack on Miss Clancey it can be classed a domestic homicide so I don't believe he'll go out and kill again. He can be bailed with restrictions imposed on him."

Within two hours the CPS made known their decision. Despite having low expectations following Frampton's explanation, Livermore was still peeved to read "it is not appropriate to charge Mr Kersher at this time."

Soon afterwards his main suspect was set free, albeit on bail, with conditions that he must surrender his passport and report to his local police station every 24 hours.

CHAPTER TWENTY-EIGHT

Friday March 15th, 2019

A relieved Kerscher spent Friday evening drinking with Keith Hopper and Philip Andrews at their old haunt, the Jolly Butcher in Bexhill.

He tried to concentrate on enjoying the rich, velvety taste of his beer but his thoughts were elsewhere.

"Cheer up, Denton," said Andrews, wiping his mouth with the back of his hand after downing a second pint as they sat on stools at the counter of the public bar.

Kerscher forced a smile and took another sip of his first pint.

Andrews patted him on the back and said: "The police have really got it in for you, haven't they?"

"Yeah, but they're completely wrong again. They think I killed Pippa and Holly simply because I went out with both of them. The fact I was found not guilty of Pippa's murder doesn't seem to make any difference to that tosser Livermore and his muppets."

"They obviously don't believe in coincidences," mused Andrews in his Scottish twang.

"That's all it is - a bloody awful coincidence. I didn't kill either of them, but they'd have charged me if it hadn't been for my old mate Keith, here."

Hopper beamed at him. "You mean me telling the fuzz you and I were still together at 11.30 on the night of Holly's murder?"

"Yeah. I'm very grateful, mate. You got me off the hook. I hadn't a clue what time I actually left you."

"Don't you remember, Denton? We spent ages chatting outside the Golden Swan. We were there so long I was able to smoke a couple of fags."

Kerscher shook his head. "I'd had a skinful so my memory's a bit hazy. It was a Godsend that you were able to give me an alibi."

Andrews took another long sip of his beer. "You deserve a break, Denton. You're an unlucky bugger."

"I bloody well am, mate. I'm still facing a sexual assault charge brought by that lying bitch Barbie Dickinson."

"What happened exactly?" Hopper wanted to know. "Did you try it on with her?"

"No, I bloody well didn't. I simply knocked on her flat door to collect a parcel she'd taken in for me. Why she accused me of touching her up I don't know."

"But something must have happened," Andrews insisted. "She's a good looker, isn't she?"

"Yes, she is. But nothing happened. I admit I had an eyeful of her tits because she was wearing a revealing top and they were almost hanging out of it. I even paid her a compliment, but I didn't touch her."

"She's got really big tits, has she?" asked Hopper, laughing.

"They're massive, mate, but she's completely off her trolley accusing me of feeling them."

"That's probably what upset her," Hopper told him, licking beer from his bottom lip. "She wanted you to touch her up and got the needle when you didn't. Maybe she was gagging for it."

***

Livermore had found it awkward explaining to senior members of his team why Kerscher was released.

He told them: "There isn't sufficient evidence regarding the murder, and the CPS don't think it advisable to charge him with making a threat to kill at this stage while our investigation is on-going."

"How do they justify making that decision, Gov?" asked DC Jones. "Wouldn't it be best to have him locked up?"

Livermore shrugged. "That's a question I asked myself, Valerie. The CPS don't believe anybody else is at risk."

"How's that?" scoffed O'Sullivan.

"It's because Kerscher made the threat to kill to someone he was involved with emotionally. The public are not considered to be at risk."

O'Sullivan guffawed.

Livermore felt the need to give a further explanation and repeated what Frampton had told him. "The powers-that-be think that if Kerscher committed the murder it was a domestic homicide and they don't believe he'll kill again."

O'Sullivan scoffed once more.

"So what's our priority now, Gov?" Dimbleby wanted to know.

"We need to continue to fully investigate Kerscher and do the same with other suspects as well."

CHAPTER TWENTY-NINE

Saturday, March 16th, 2019

Livermore had misgivings when Frampton informed him there would be a Press conference at 11am on Saturday.

Just before it started, Livermore expressed one of his concerns to his 'superior'. "Have you seen Gerald Truelove's story in today's paper, sir? He's claiming that the police don't know whether members of the public are under threat from one or two murderers."

Frampton told him: "I suggest you say 'no comment' if that comes up, Harvey. I will leave you to answer questions after I've made an appeal for information."

A room full of reporters and cameramen were assembled to hear Frampton make his appeal to the public.

He said: "We are asking anyone who may have heard or seen anything in relation to the murder of Holly Clancey to come forward. Local businesses should check their CCTV for the relevant times."

Frampton then gave details of how Holly had been driving home on Wednesday night prior to being murdered in her apartment. He explained that her car had broken down and she had presumably completed her journey on foot.

Livermore was far from happy when Frampton, having

completed the easy part of the conference, handed over to him.

"Have you found the murder weapon?" asked a female reporter from one of the nationals.

He felt obliged to give the standard answer: "I am unable to provide that information at this stage as it could be to the detriment of our investigation."

"Did the killer leave any prints or DNA?" queried a member of the Sky TV team.

Livermore was again non-committal. "We're still waiting for a full forensics report to be completed."

"I understand you arrested Denton Kerscher on suspicion of murder, but have released him without charge," said a reporter who was partly hidden from Livermore's view by a camera in front of him. But the surly voice was unmistakably that of Gerald Truelove. "Can you explain that, Chief Inspector?"

Livermore side-stepped the question by replying: "It is not our policy to release names of potential suspects. I can confirm a male suspect was arrested and interviewed and has been 'released under investigation' which is not unusual in enquiries of this nature."

Truelove was not satisfied. "Kerscher was found not guilty of murdering another woman, Pippa Mercer, in May 2017. Do you think the public needs to be protected from this man?"

Livermore's face reddened but he managed to appear unruffled. "I have no comment to make about Mr Kerscher.

If we were aware of a general or specific risk to members of the public we would advise accordingly."

"Can you confirm what was taken from the crime scene?" Truelove wanted to know, stepping from behind the camera.

Livermore looked at him blankly, so the reporter explained: "When Pippa Mercer was murdered the killer took her panties. Did the same thing happen with Holly Clancey?

There were murmurs among the assembled media representatives as Livermore replied: "As an experienced reporter, Mr Truelove, you no doubt appreciate that it would not be prudent for the police to release information that could potentially prejudice an investigation so I am somewhat surprised you raise such a question."

A middle-aged female reporter called Maria waved her hand furiously to attract the policeman's attention.

"I'll take one last question," said Livermore. "Yes, Maria?"

"Do you think Pippa Mercer and Holly Clancey were killed by the same man?"

"We are conducting a full and detailed investigation and it would be inappropriate to make any such assumptions at this stage. Any conclusions we reach in due course will be based on the evidence we are presented with."

On receiving a nod from Frampton, a disgruntled Livermore rose to his feet. "That brings this Press conference to a close. As DCS Frampton has already said, it would be helpful if anyone who heard of saw anything in relation to the murder of Holly Clancey contacts us. That also applies to anyone who knew Miss Clancey and might have information about her. Thank you all for coming."

CHAPTER THIRTY

Sunday, March 17th, 2019

Livermore and Evelyne were awoken from their slumbers in their stylish detached house in Saltdean by a loud crash downstairs.

"What the devil's that?" his startled wife shouted, putting on her bedside light.

The first thing Livermore's eyes focused on was the alarm clock showing 5.46am. Before he could answer they heard another shattering noise.

This time Livermore was sufficiently awake to become aware that glass was being smashed.

"Bloody hell!" he yelled. "Some bastard is breaking our windows."

He jumped out of bed as a third window was struck.

Running downstairs in his bare feet and pyjamas, Livermore opened the front door and peered along the drive leading to a quiet tree-lined road. But there was no sight of the vandal - just the sound of someone running in the distance.

Evelyne turned on the lounge light to survey the damage. On seeing what little was left of the windows and a mass of broken glass covering the floor, she burst into tears and began to tremble.

Harvey took her in his arms and said soothingly: "There, there, my darling. It's all over now."

"Is it, Harvey?"

"Yes, the bugger has run off."

"But we can't be sure he won't come back, can we?"

It was a prospect Livermore dreaded.

***

Livermore found that three bricks had done the damage and called out colleagues to examine them.

By the time the mess had been cleared up, the DSI felt drained. A strong coffee helped to revive him and he discussed the situation with Nottage.

"Have you got any idea who might have done it, Gov?"

"A few cons I helped put away come to mind, but I don't think they'd go that far," Livermore admitted.

Nottage suggested an alternative scenario. "Perhaps it was some nutter who picked out a house at random. Hopefully, he's left some evidence behind."

CHAPTER THIRTY-ONE

Monday, March 18th, 2019

Livermore's misery continued when he read Monday morning's newspapers.

Gerald Truelove had run a story headlined 'Have police got it wrong again?'

The journalist revealed DSI Harvey Livermore and his Major Crime team had made Denton Kerscher the 'main person of interest' in the murder of Holly Clancey, but released him without charge.

The story stressed that Kerscher had been found not guilty of the previous murder of Pippa Mercer, and suggested police might again be focusing on the wrong man.

Even more damaging was a post made on social media by a 56-year-old computer programmer called Judith Stenning. Prior to remarrying, she had been Judith Kerscher and was Denton's mother.

She claimed her son was being victimised by the police and two papers quoted her.

Mrs Stenning said: "My son isn't a killer - he's a victim. Not content with taking him to court for one murder and seeing the case dismissed, the police are now accusing him of a second murder without any evidence.

"Denton is not violent. He's actually a sensitive man

who loves beauty, art and literature. Like me, he does not suffer fools gladly and strives for perfection, which perhaps explains why his relationships with his two girlfriends ended. But he is kind and thoughtful.

"Hopefully the police will find the real killer and leave my son to get on with his life. Denton has suffered enough."

Truelove did not go as far as Mrs Stenning, but he claimed police still had no idea if they were looking for one man or two. To back this up he referred to the DCI saying it would be inappropriate to make any assumptions at this stage.

Livermore swore. "That bloody reporter! He's used only part of my comment to make it fit his wild accusations."

Another paper ran an editorial saying: "Police are not telling us anything - we've a right to know if the man they arrested and let go is a possible threat to the public."

**

Fussy Frampton summoned Livermore for another 'chat' and immediately referred to that day's papers laying across his imposing Rosewood desk.

"I've already read them, sir," a fed-up Livermore told him. "They've distorted the facts."

He then had to suffer the indignity of listening to Frampton sounding off at him. "The media are even suggesting we're victimising Kerscher," the DCI stormed. "I thought the Press conference would defuse the situation - not make it worse."

"Any accusation of victimisation is rubbish, sir. Unfortunately, Kerscher's mother has made an emotional statement - she'd have everyone believe he's a saint."

"But it doesn't look good, does it, Harvey? And we don't seem to be getting anywhere with this case, do we?"

"I beg to differ, sir. I think we're making reasonable progress."

Frampton peered at him over the top of his horn-rimmed glasses while glancing again at one of the newspaper headlines. "Does that mean we now know if the murders of Pippa Mercer and Holly Clancey were committed by one man or two?"

Livermore tried to give himself some wriggle room. "Unfortunately, forensics have not come up with any evidence so far."

"That's not much help to residents who want to know if they have one or two killers in their midst, is it Harvey?"

Frampton twirled his pen around in his right hand and gave what Livermore took to be a disapproving look.

"We hope to have the answer soon, sir. It would help if you can provide me with more manpower."

Frampton snorted. "I only wish I could, Harvey. But the Government are spending more on foreign aid than on policing."

Livermore remained silent because he knew this to be true. Frampton continued: "You've shown in the past that you've got excellent powers of detection, Harvey. What is your 'take' on these murders - do you believe they were committed by the same man?"

"Yes, sir, I do. Our profiler Ralph Vickers thinks they were both carried out by a deeply disturbed individual and I agree with him. In both cases the murderer seems to have lost his temper and resorted to making a frenzied attack. But I believe he was also sexually attracted to the two victims. As you know, he took their panties, apparently as a trophy or to use to pleasure himself."

"And do you still think that Denton Kerscher is the killer?"

Livermore was reluctant to fully commit himself. "The fact Kerscher was going out with both victims makes him an obvious suspect. And Barbie Dickinson's claim that he sexually assaulted her increases my suspicions even further. But the latest search of his flat has failed to uncover Miss Clancey's panties or anything else incriminating and one of his friends says they were outside a pub together at the time of the second murder.

"We do have other suspects. One is Miss Clancey's most recent boyfriend Rodney Plowright and another is her employer Fabio Camaggio, who's faced sexual harassment cases which have cost him a small fortune to settle.

"There's also a 'charmer' named Jawad Zirak, who has two convictions for sex attacks and took his victims' panties as a trophy the second time. Further inquiries have just revealed that some of Zirak's relatives in Manchester are suspected of being part of a sex gang which raped and trafficked white victims. But there's nothing so far to suggest that he was a member of this gang."

"Well, try to speed up the process, Harvey, because some people in high places are suggesting that the media know more about the case than we do. It would be most unfortunate if my superiors decided to bring in someone else to run the case."

CHAPTER THIRTY-TWO

Monday, March 18th, 2019

Livermore called another meeting of his team.

"Right," he said, "has anyone got any good news for me?"

Nobody spoke. "Let me rephrase that - does anyone have any news, good or bad?"

"Yeah," said O'Sullivan, "Jeff has a good case for suing his barber."

This brought laughter all round and a smile from Livermore as he saw his second-in-command wince. Nottage retaliated by saying: "You're a fine one to talk, Mike. At least I've still got some hair, mate."

There were a few more chuckles as eyes turned to O'Sullivan and his bald patch.

Livermore held up his hand for silence. "OK, OK, let's get down to the more serious business of this murder investigation. We'll start with Jawad Zirak. Have we questioned him?"

"Yes, Guv," said O'Sullivan. "DC Valerie Jones and I have been to see him at a house in Brighton which he's been sharing with six other Pakistanis for the last 12 months. Zirak can't account for where he was when the first murder occurred, but reckons he's just finished working on a building site in Colchester. He says he spent two weeks there, including the time of the second murder. We're still checking that because the building firm which carried out the work have no record of him."

"So he could be in the frame," enthused Livermore.

"Maybe," said O'Sullivan, "but I don't want to raise any false hopes. The builders claim they sub-contracted some of the work to another outfit who took on labourers on a cash-in-hand basis. Zirak could have been one of them. I've spoken to the CID in Colchester and they're making inquiries, but nothing's come up so..."

Nottage cut in: "If Zirak's telling the truth, it shouldn't take long to find out which doss house he stayed in."

"No such luck," moaned O'Sullivan. "Zirak says he was so short of cash he slept rough while he was in Colchester."

"For the whole two weeks?" asked Dimbleby. "I wouldn't have fancied working with him. He must have stunk like a skunk."

"And you'd know all about good hygiene, wouldn't you, Chris?" chided O'Sullivan. "Zirak claims he slept in a sports ground near the building site. He reckons it was easy to break in and he slept in a changing room where he could wash each day. Anyway, Colchester CID are checking with CCTV cameras. We've searched the house in Brighton, but so far we've got nothing to place him anywhere near Miss Clancey's home."

"That's not conclusive," said Livermore, trying to curb his impatience. "We can only rule him out if he was actually seen in Colchester on the day of the murder.

"I've been sharing information with police in Manchester about some of Zirak's relatives being in a gang suspected of raping and trafficking white women. They have nothing on him, but then they've dragged their feet about the whole sad situation up there because of fears of racism. So we'll keep a very close eye on Mr Zirak. Let's start by talking to the two women he was convicted of sexually assaulting previously. The fact he took one victim's panties as a trophy makes him a real suspect."

There were nods and murmurs of agreement.

Livermore had another thought. "What size shoes does Zirak take, Mike?"

"Tens, Gov. The same size as one of the footprints outside Miss Clancey's apartment, but he only seems to own a single pair and they've got cement and other building muck all over them."

Livermore moved on. "We've checked the shoes belonging to Denton Kerscher and Fabio Camaggio without any luck, but I understand Rodney Plowright wears size tens with soles similar to those we're looking for. Is there anything more on him?"

Chris brought his boss up to date. "Yes, Gov. Plowright claims he got home about eight o'clock on the night Miss Clancey was killed, but I've spoken to his neighbours and none of them saw him."

Conteh waved her arm to attract Livermore's attention.

"Yes Grace."

"I've been going through Miss Clancey's phone calls and messages. There were several from Plowright. He was obviously very keen on her, and sent her a couple of suggestive texts.

"I've also looked at her Facebook messages and there were some very cheeky ones from a guy called Kyle Carter, who describes himself as a keen photographer when not working for the NHS. It turns out that Miss Clancey once modelled for a local camera club at which Carter is a member. He kept in touch with her on Facebook. In one message he told her she looked fit but should let him check her over in his capacity as a medical consultant. That's taking exaggeration to a new level - he's actually a porter at Eastbourne Hospital."

"A bit of a Walter Mitty," said Livermore.

"He could be a sexual predator," Conteh insisted. "Another of his Facebook messages told Holly he had some great pictures of her and he'd like to give her one."

The room erupted in laughter.

"OK, Grace. Let's find out more about him. We also need to talk to the parents of both Holly Clancey and Pippa Mercer again. They've already said they don't think their daughters knew each other, but is it possible both victims had any connections to these latest suspects?"

CHAPTER THIRTY-THREE

Monday, March 18th, 2019

The party was in full swing and host Ricky Payne was in the kitchen snorting a line of coke when the sounds hit him.

Ricky, a transvestite wearing a woman's wig, miniskirt and high-heels, could hear ringing, followed by banging, above the noise of music blaring out from the lounge.

He knew the cocaine would give him an immediate rush but it had never affected him like this before.

Only after further ringing and banging did he realise that the noises were not in his head. Someone was hammering on his front door and repeatedly pressing the bell.

"Damn!" muttered the lanky 30-year-old cross-dresser. He quickly scraped the remainder of the white powder on to his right palm and brushed it into a pot in the kitchen cupboard.

"What's up, darling?" asked his effeminate friend Lennie.

"Some fucker's bashing the bloody door in. It could be the Filth."

The bell rang again. Ricky cursed, pushed past a group of gyrating guests in the lounge of his crowded flat and hurried to open the front door.

He was relieved to find it was not the police - but a couple in their Sixties. Both had grim looks on their faces.

For a few seconds they stared at each other in stunned silence.

Ricky was the first to speak. "Sorry, if we're making too much noise," he blurted out.

The man in front of him, with thinning grey hair, parted neatly, told him: "We're not here to complain about the noise - it actually helped us find your flat. We're here to collect our daughter Rachel."

"Rachel?"

"Yes, Rachel Goldberg. She told us she was coming to a party in this block."

Ricky, exhaling through pursed lips painted bright red, still looked puzzled.

The petite woman added sharply: "Rachel's only 15, but looks older. She said she'd be home by mid-night and it's now gone one."

"Ah," beamed Ricky, finally twigging who they were talking about. "I remember her. But I think she left about 15 minutes ago with Kyle."

"Who's Kyle?" the grey-haired, portly man demanded.

"Kyle Carter."

"And where can we find this Kyle Carter?" demanded the man.

"Let me check to see if his car is still here."

Ricky pushed past them, wobbled on to the balcony in his four-inch heels and peered over the metal barrier at the parking area below.

"His car's down there. It's a blue Skoda."

***

Mr and Mrs Goldberg hurried down two flights of steps and crossed a tarmacked area in which about thirty cars were parked. As they approached the Skoda, they could hear noises coming from inside it.

An angry Mr Goldberg pulled open the rear nearside door and saw a trouserless man, with a ponytail, on top of a nearly naked girl. It was his daughter.

"Get off her!" he yelled, grabbing the panting man's long hair and yanking it so viciously that the headband snapped.

The man and the girl both yelped - him in pain and her in shock

"Dad!" she cried, trying to cover up her exposed breasts with her hands. She had red bite marks around her neck and on her chest.

Seeing the marks, a disgusted Mr Goldberg slammed his fist into Carter's chubby face and shouted to his wife: "Call the police."

***

An hour later the police, having responded to Mrs Goldberg's 999 call, had arrested Kyle Carter and taken him into custody.

CHAPTER THIRTY-FOUR

Tuesday, March 19th, 2019

Livermore was in Eastbourne Hospital, keeping his 8.30am outpatient appointment with Dr Morgan in Respiratory medicine.

"Good morning," the middle-aged, amiable specialist greeted him as Livermore lowered himself into a chair. "I've received the result of your PET scan and it reveals two small objects in your right lung. Let me show you what they look like."

He pointed to a picture of Livermore's lung on the screen in front of him which revealed two shadows.

"Are they cancerous?" his anxious patient wanted to know.

"They could be. The good news is that it's not spread to anywhere else on your body so if we remove part of your lung then you'll be rid of it."

"How much of the lung?" Livermore queried.

"Probably one lobe. But the results of the breathing test we gave you are pretty good so it should not be a problem."

They exchanged grim smiles. "What do you recommend, doctor?"

"I think you should see a surgeon with a view to having an operation. But, if you prefer, we could wait six months, then give you another scan to see if the objects in your lung have grown or remained the same size. At this stage we can't be sure they are cancerous but it's likely."

An agitated Livermore cracked his knuckles. "What's the greater risk - waiting or having an operation now?"

"There's always a risk with any surgery, but for an otherwise fit man of 46 years old, like yourself, it should not prove a problem," Morgan told him, stroking the designer stubble on his chin. "Modern VATS surgery means it's a minimally invasive technique. On the other hand, if you don't have the operation and we later find you've got cancer then it could have spread."

The normally decisive policeman found it hard to make a decision. Dr Morgan told him: "Let me arrange an appointment with a surgeon - you can make up your mind when you see him."

When Livermore got back to his office he looked up VATS on his computer and discovered what it was - video-assisted thoracoscopic surgery.

"Sounds like some bloody robot would be cutting into me," he said out loud to himself.

He pondered the situation. The problem was, even if an operation went well, he would probably need a month to recover.

Common sense told the worried policeman he should have the surgery as soon as possible, but there were two factors against that. He was in the middle of a murder investigation and felt he could not walk away from it.

Secondly, he couldn't bear to be stuck at home recovering while at the 'mercy' of his over-protective, nagging wife.

CHAPTER THIRTY-FIVE

Tuesday, March 19th, 2019

Livermore received an unexpected telephone call from DCI Lucinda Monahan at Eastbourne CID.

She informed him that a 28-year-old man had just been charged with indecent assault on a 15-year-old girl. "You may have an interest in him," she added in her thick Irish brogue. "His name is Kyle Carter."

Livermore's previously grim expression changed into a smile and he switched on the charm. "Yes, Lucinda. You are quite right. Mr Carter is most certainly of interest to us."

"I thought so," Monahan repeated. "I saw on the computer that you want to question him in connection with the murder of Holly Clancey. We have him in one of our cells. Would you like to come over to Eastbourne to interview him?"

So the distraught hospital porter found himself facing more questions, this time from Livermore and Nottage in the stark, 12ft square interview room at Eastbourne Police Station.

"Look," said the clearly worried Carter, "I don't want to say anything more. I was caught with the girl in the back of my car, but I didn't force myself on her - she consented to everything."

Studying the overweight, puffy-cheeked, ponytailed figure in front of him, Livermore found that hard to believe.

"I shouldn't have been charged," continued Carter, starting to shake uncontrollably.

The DCI, sensing that the man might be on the verge of breaking down, adopted a softer approach than he had originally intended.

"You've been charged with sexual assault because the girl was under the age of 16. It doesn't matter if she consented. But that is not what we want to talk to you about, Mr Carter. There is another matter which we can deal with now or do so later if you prefer to have a solicitor present."

"Are you charging me with something else?" Carter asked.

"No, at this stage we just want to ask you some questions about a young lady called Holly Clancey. We understand you knew her."

"I may have done," the man replied noncommittally. "I'm not sure."

"Well, let me refresh your memory, Mr Carter. You sent her messages on Facebook."

"I send loads of people Facebook messages - that doesn't mean I know them."

"You knew Miss Clancey," Nottage said firmly. "Our inquiries show that you are a member of a camera club at which Holly posed for pictures."

"Ah, now I remember. Yeah, me and other members took pictures of her when she came to one of our meetings as a model."

Nottage persisted. "And you sent her some very saucy messages on Facebook."

"She accepted my request to be a Facebook 'friend' and we exchanged messages. But that's all. I didn't really know her."

"So you did not have a relationship with her?"

"No." Carter shook his head, causing his ponytail to swing from left to right.

Livermore took over the questioning. "Are you aware that Miss Clancey was murdered on Wednesday, March 13th?"

"Yeah, I read about it in the papers."

"And where were you on that night?"

"At work. I'm a porter at Eastbourne Hospital and I was on nights last week."

"What hours did you work?" the DCI wanted to know.

"From 8.45pm to 6am so there's no way I could have had anything to do with her murder."

CHAPTER THIRTY-SIX

Wednesday, March 20th, 2019

Another meeting of the Operation Flamingo team began with some major disappointments for Livermore.

He ignored the coffee he had made for himself as O'Sullivan kicked things off by delivering the first of them.

"The search of Jawad Zirak's home in Brighton revealed nothing, Gov, apart from some goods he's probably nicked. Worse still, I've just heard from the CID in Colchester. They've found that someone on the building site remembers a young Asian called Jawad working there. CCTV also places him in the town centre in Colchester on the night of Miss Clancey's murder."

"So that puts paid to him as a suspect," lamented Livermore. "Is there anything on our over-friendly estate agent Rodney Plowright, our lecherous employer Fabio Camaggio and our Walter Mittty hospital porter Kyle Carter?"

Nottage started to rise to his feet, but analyst Helen Yates spoke first. "I've checked Plowright's mobile phone records," she said with a toothy smile. "He made a great deal of calls."

"And do any of them tie him into the murder?" asked Livermore, trying to show patience, even though he wanted to urge her to get to the point.

The smile and the teeth vanished. "No, sir. Just the opposite. Mr Plowright was making a call on his mobile at his home, or near to it, around the time Miss Clancey was murdered."

Livermore groaned inwardly. "Has anyone got any good news?"

Nottage began climbing to his feet again, but this time was beaten to it by Dimbleby. "I've something here that may be helpful," the veteran copper said, waving a white envelope from which he took out a large photograph.

O'Sullivan could not resist taunting: "We haven't time to look at your family snaps, Chris."

Dimbleby ignored him. "This came in the post today, addressed to me, from an anonymous source. It's a picture of Fabio Camaggio with his arm round Holly Clancey. It seems to disprove his claim that he hardly knew her."

"Any idea why it was sent to you, Chris?" asked Livermore, taking the picture from him.

"Probably because I gave out my card to several of Camaggio's employees - one of them is trying to tell us something. You'll see on the back of the photo that it's the copyright of the Eastbourne Herald - it bears their stamp. I checked with the Herald this morning and discovered the picture was taken at an exhibition of modern and contemporary art at the Towner Gallery two months ago."

Livermore gave his first smile of the day. "So it would appear Camaggio might have known Miss Clancey very well indeed. You'll need to have further words with him, Chris."

Nottage at last stood up and spoke. "There's better news regarding Kyle Carter."

"Let's hear it, then, Jeff."

"A fellow member of his camera club has said that Carter seemed to be infatuated with Miss Clancey. We've also spoken to some of Carter's work-mates and apparently it was not unusual for him to go missing during shifts at the hospital. One of the nurses was very forthcoming. She told us Carter appeared to have problems with his former live-in girlfriend, who actually received treatment in the hospital on one occasion for injuries he may have inflicted. The ex-girlfriend's name is Hazel Tweedy. When I find her current address I'll pay her a visit."

This brought a look of approval from Livermore. "That sounds very promising."

But Nottage had some bad news, too. "I've done some extensive checking on whether Camaggio or Plowright had any connection with Pippa Mercer as well as Holly Clancey. But I've not come up with anything so far. Plowright's mobile record seems to have ruled him out as a suspect for Holly's murder anyway - unless someone else was using his mobile."

Livermore finally noticed his coffee. He took a sip but it was as cold as some of the leads they had. *'Surely'*, he thought, *'things are going to take a turn for the better soon'*.

CHAPTER THIRTY-SEVEN

Thursday, March 21st, 2019

Barbie Dickinson paid Gavin Johnson a surprise visit at his recently decorated flat.

She felt incredibly sexy in red stiletto heeled shoes, skin-tight black jeggings and a figure-hugging white jacket.

As they sat on a two-seater sofa, drinking coffee, Barbie flashed him a big smile and complimented him on the new colour scheme of pale blue and cream he had chosen for his lounge.

"The flat's in great shape - and so are you," Barbie told him, gazing lovingly at his well-toned body. "Have you been working out?"

"Yeah. I still go down the gym regularly. What about you, Barbie? How are you feeling, following the attack?"

"I'm fully recovered, how do I look?"

"Good."

"Good? Is that all?" she asked with a teasing smile. "Perhaps you should make a closer inspection, Gav."

The tantalising teenager unzipped her short jacket. She was wearing nothing underneath and her large 38D breasts tumbled out.

"Do you like what you see, Gav?" Then she stood up and twirled around provocatively. "What do you think of my new jeggings? They're so tight I've had to go commando."

She was expecting Johnson's handsome face to register pleasure, arousal and desire. But she didn't see it.

"What's the matter, baby?" she asked. "We haven't had a shag for ages. So come here and give me a good fucking."

"Look, Barbie," he said in a strained voice, while remaining seated. "I explained to you months ago that our relationship wasn't working. I don't think us having sex is going to put things right."

Her mood changed dramatically.

"You bastard!" she screeched, angrily zipping up her jacket. "How can you treat me like this after all I've been through?"

Gavin finally stood up so that his 6ft 2in frame towered over her. "I've tried to help and support you following the assault, but we were no longer an item, and we can't just become one again."

She lashed out with her right hand to slap him, but he parried the blow.

"I'm sorry," he said.

"Being sorry's not enough, is it? I thought the fact some other bloke was lusting after me would make you see what you were missing. I've done everything I could to win you back, Gav. Even lied to the police."

"What do you mean?" he demanded.

"Never mind."

"Are you saying that bloke never attacked you?"

She didn't answer. But her face reddened noticeably before she turned and stormed out of the flat.

***

A heartbroken Barbie spent the next few hours at home moping, sobbing and guzzling wine.

Her misery was coupled with fear. The court date for her to give evidence against Denton Kerscher was fast approaching and she was dreading it.

In a panic she searched through her bag and found the phone number that had been provided by the Sexual Offences Liaison Officer Pauline James. Barbie's shaking hands caused her to twice dial incorrectly before getting though.

Pauline's friendly voice was encouraging, and Barbie blurted out: "He didn't do it."

"Who didn't do what, Barbie?"

"I'm talking about that guy."

"What guy, Barbie?"

"You know...that bloke Kerscher. He had a good look at my tits - a real good look - but he didn't touch them."

"You told us he squeezed one of them so hard he caused it to become swollen. We took pictures showing the bruising and swelling."

There was a long silence.

"Barbie?"

"I caused the bruise myself. I did it."

"You also told us that Mr Kerscher indecently exposed himself to you. Was that true?"

There was another long silence. Finally Pauline repeated: "Did he expose himself to you, Barbie?"

"No."

"Why did you tell us he did?"

"I dunno."

"You must have had a reason, Barbie. Had you met Denton Kerscher previously?"

"No. I'd read about him assaulting his former girlfriend outside a nightclub and after he'd stared at my tits it gave me the idea to say he'd assaulted me, too."

"But why?"

"My boyfriend Gavin and I had split up. It was Valentine's Day and nobody had sent me a card. I wanted to get Gav back."

"How did you think claiming you'd been assaulted by Denton Kerscher would achieve that?"

"It meant I could ring Gav and ask him to help me. It would also show him how desirable I was to another man. Gav came round immediately, just as I planned. I had ripped my top and squeezed my breast until it became swollen to convince him I'd been assaulted. How was I to know the silly sod would phone the police?"

CHAPTER THIRTY-EIGHT

Thursday, March 21st, 2019

Stand-up Buddy Brown was going down well at the Comedy Club in Eastbourne.

He knew this audience liked his warm personality and risqué jokes. And he had them rocking with laughter when he told them: "I went out with this gorgeous girl. She had everything - unfortunately I've got it now!"

After finishing his act he had a drink at the bar where he lapped up the praise of a couple of female punters.

"You were great, Buddy," one of them told him. "Can we have your autograph?"

"Sure," he said, treating her to a big smile as he admired her good looks.

The women handed him leaflets showing his picture which they had collected from the foyer.

"What are your names?" he asked, starting to write personalised messages to each of them.

"Tessa and Gwen," said the taller of the two, whose slender figure he was taking an interest in. "I'm Tessa. You've become a regular in Eastbourne, haven't you?"

"Yeah, I first performed here three years ago and I've been invited back twice so I must be doing something right."

The dapper, middle-aged comedian handed back the signed leaflets and looked at the shorter, fuzzy-haired woman more closely. "I think I remember you."

"Yes, my friend Pippa Mercer and I met you here once before. You took her out, didn't you?"

"Pippa?" he queried.

"Yes, she was a blonde, Welsh girl in her twenties."

"Ah, yes. I remember her. She was a real looker - similar to the girl I joked about tonight. She had everything."

His sly grin was not returned by Gwen, who told him: "Pippa was killed soon after she went out with you. She was murdered."

Buddy's demeanour abruptly changed. "What are you getting at?" he snapped.

"Nothing," gasped the woman.

Buddy tried to cover up his agitation with a false smile, but it was clearly too late to appease Gwen.

CHAPTER THIRTY-NINE

Friday, March 22nd, 2019

Barbie had been horrified to be told that she might be charged, or at least cautioned, for wasting police time.

But on Friday she arranged an evening out with her friend Annie to give herself a much-needed pick-me-up. And Barbie readily agreed when Annie suggested: "Let's go to a club and pull a couple of blokes."

As she got ready by showering and towelling herself down, Barbie sang 'I'm Gonna Wash That Man Right Out of My Hair.' Then she strolled into the bedroom and admired the smoothness of her long, slender legs in the wall mirror.

'You look alright, girl!'

Her thoughts were interrupted by a noise outside. "It must be that bloody stray cat again," she said to herself, putting on red panties and matching suspender belt.

She found a pair of white stockings in a draw and took her time gently pulling them up each leg before fastening the tops to her suspenders.

The attractive young woman then slipped into a pair of designer slippers with heels and enjoyed another appreciative look at herself in the mirror. This time she inspected her ample breasts and muttered: "That stupid fool Gav doesn't appreciate what he's missing."

Barbie resumed singing but was disturbed by another sound from outside the window.

She glanced through the slightly parted curtains and was alarmed to see a man's face staring back at her.

She screamed - and he fled!

***

Worried that the Peeping Tom might be waiting for her outside, Barbie phoned the police.

The Station Officer said her complaint would be looked into, and he'd ask a patrol car driver to see if anyone was loitering near her home.

But he admitted there was not much more the police could do as she hadn't recognised the man and could only vaguely describe him.

***

"Just look at this," O'Sullivan said to Conteh as she passed his desk.

She peered over his shoulder at the item on his computer screen, but he gave her the details anyway.

"That bloody woman Barbie Dickinson who wasted our time with her lies about Kerscher supposedly assaulting her is now claiming she's the victim of a voyeur."

Conteh read the brief report. "Perhaps she's telling the truth this time," she said.

O'Sullivan scoffed. "Come off it, Grace. She makes this

sort of stuff up to get her kicks. And whereas most Peepers spy on women getting undressed, she claims this guy watched her get dressed."

Before Conteh could respond again, her arrogant colleague continued to spout off his opinion. "I've got better things to do than listen to the allegations of a bird-brained, sex-mad attention seeker."

CHAPTER FORTY

Tuesday, March 26th, 2019

"Come in!" called Livermore as Nottage gave his usual double knock on the office door. "What have you got for me, Jeff?"

Nottage sat down and told his boss: "A couple of things have occurred that could be linked to the case, Guv. Firstly, a woman called Gwen Wiggins has informed us that Buddy Brown, a stand-up comedian, went out with Pippa Mercer round about the time she was murdered."

Livermore was puzzled. "Why has it taken her all this time to come forward?"

"Gwen and her friend went to see his latest performance at a comedy club last week and talked to him in the bar afterwards. She says that Buddy Brown got the needle when she reminded him about his date with Pippa. He suddenly changed from Mr Nice Guy to Mr Nasty and she thought it seemed suspicious. Apparently, Holly Clancey liked going to comedy shows, too. So she may have had contact with Mr Brown as well."

"It's certainly worth checking out, Jeff. Let's see what Buddy Brown has to say for himself. Get someone to pay him a visit."

"I'll probably do it myself, Guv. The other thing that has

cropped up is rather odd. Philip Andrews has gone missing."

Livermore looked at his colleague blankly. "Philip Andrews? Should I know him?"

"He's one of Denton Kerscher's two best mates. Andrews and Keith Hopper are Kerscher's regular drinking companions."

"What do you mean when you say he's gone missing?"

"Andrews' wife Mary has been on the phone to us twice and made a report. She's not seen him since Sunday."

"Perhaps he's gone on a bender - or left her."

"Maybe, Gov. But Mrs Andrews says nothing like this has ever happened in 25 years of marriage. And in the last three days her husband hasn't used a credit card or drawn money out of his bank account."

"OK. We'll give it some priority. Ask Dimbley and Conteh to find out when Andrews was last seen. We need to talk to his work colleagues and friends - especially Mr Kerscher."

The phone rang on Livermore's desk and, upon answering it, he heard his wife sobbing at the other end of the line.

"What on earth's the matter, Evelyne?" he asked. "What's happened?"

"It's dreadful, Harvey. Someone's thrown red paint all over my car."

"They've done what?"

"Some lunatic has covered my lovely blue car with red

paint. I parked it in a side road while I was in my hairdresser's and I've just returned to find it ruined."

Livermore managed to control his anger as he found suitable words of comfort for his wife.

Amid more sobs, she blurted out: "It's obviously the same person who smashed our windows. Can't you find him?"

"Don't worry, I will," he assured her. "This time there should be a witness or CTTV to place him near to your car."

***

Livermore arranged for a friend of Evelyne's to pick up his distressed wife.

Nottage, having overhead everything, instructed two PCs to investigate if anyone had seen this latest act of vandalism.

He then asked Livermore to draw up list of villains who might have a personal score to settle against him.

CHAPTER FORTY-ONE

Wednesday, March 27th, 2019

Conteh and Dimbleby discovered that the 47-year-old Philip Andrews had few friends apart from Kerscher and Hopper.

His colleagues at the warehouse in which he worked said they did not mix with him socially and they'd not seen or heard from him during the last three days.

The two officers found it difficult to interview Mary Andrews in her plainly furnished lounge because she kept breaking down, sobbing. "I can't understand it," she muttered, wiping away tears. "Our car is still in the garage so where could Phil have gone?"

Conteh tried to gently coax the woman to provide some details. "When was the last time you actually saw your husband?" she asked.

"After lunch on Sunday. He walked down to the pub as usual. But he never returned." This recollection brought more tears.

"Do you remember what he was wearing?"

"Yes. His usual three-quarter length dark grey coat."

"What else?" pressed Conteh "Can you recall?"

"He'd put on a light blue shirt and dark blue trousers I'd ironed for him that morning."

Conteh, aware that Dimbleby was happy for her to continue the questioning, said: "What time did you expect Phil to come back?"

"I assumed he was making a night of it with his pals so I went to bed and fell asleep. When I woke up on Monday morning to find he hadn't come home I was frantic with worry. I telephoned Phil's mother and she was just as shocked as me, although the stuck-up cow couldn't resist suggesting he'd probably left me. But we hadn't had a row and he didn't pack a bag or say anything about going away."

"What about other family members and friends - did you check with them? "Your son or daughter?" queried Dimbleby.

"We have no children. I rang everyone I could think of, but nobody knew where he was. That's when I contacted the police station."

There were further sobs which led to Conteh giving the distressed Mrs Andrews a hug.

At close quarters, the policewoman noted that everything about the short, dark-haired, middle-aged Mary was plain, including the frames of her glasses which dangled on a black cord around her neck.

Conteh asked: "Is there anywhere you can think of that Phil could have gone? Perhaps a favourite place you and he might have visited?"

"No. We did stay with his brother Duncan and his wife Lorraine for a week in Aberdeen last year, but I've spoken to them and they haven't heard from him in weeks."

"What about places nearer to home?" Conteh suggested.

"We didn't go out much, luv."

"Presumably you went on day trips or to the cinema and restaurants."

This prompted Mrs Andrews to actually laugh - albeit ironically. "That wasn't Phil's thing. We did go to a restaurant recently but that was because it was our wedding anniversary. We had no social life."

"So what did you usually do?" Dimbleby wanted to know.

"Phil would help me with the shopping, and we'd occasionally go for a walk. Otherwise we'd just stay in, watching TV or reading our books. Phil used to restore furniture for a hobby but that was some time ago - his main interests were watching football on TV, doing a bit of gardening and going to the pub."

Dimbleby persevered: "Did you visit any other relatives or friends who might have heard from your husband?"

"No. We haven't any close relatives apart from Phil's brother Duncan."

"And friends?"

"Phil's only real friends were Denton Kerscher and Keith Hopper. They were the first people I contacted, but they say the last time they saw him was at the weekend. Do you think he might have had an accident - or been hit by a car?"

"Nothing's been reported," said Conteh.

Dimbleby wasn't so reassuring. "Did he show an

interest in one of your women friends?"

"Come off it, luv!" scoffed Mrs Andrews. "Who'd want him?" She went on: "He's no Tom Cruise, is he? And his smoking and boozing leave a smell that would put most women off."

Conteh suppressed a laugh.

Mrs Andrews readily consented to Dimbleby and Conteh taking away her husband's computer. "It won't do you much good - he didn't use it very often."

***

They left the modest terraced house without learning anything useful about the missing Scotsman.

"It's hard to fathom," said Conteh, making a few notes after they got into their car. "His wife seems to be devoted to him despite her put-downs - she would surely have suspected something if he was planning to leave her. And for him to go off without taking anything with him doesn't make sense."

Dimbleby agreed. "Even if he had got fed up with their unexciting, uninteresting, unremarkable life together, he doesn't seem the sort to do anything on impulse, does he?"

"Too cautious, you mean?"

"Probably for the same reason nobody would bother to murder or kidnap him - he's too bloody boring!"

"Very funny, Chris! But this is not a laughing matter - since Philip Andrews went missing no payments have been taken from his credit card so he could be seriously injured or even dead."

CHAPTER FORTY-TWO

Wednesday, March 27th, 2019

Conteh switched roles with Dimbleby when they called in the Golden Swan to question customers and the landlord, a short, bearded man called Tom Hanks, who looked nothing like his film star namesake.

This time she was content to let her colleague do most of the talking as Hanks and an old soak known as Lefty confirmed that they had last seen Philip Andrews when he came in for a drink on Sunday afternoon.

"Was he here long?" Dimbleby wanted to know.

"No," said Hanks, while washing a couple of glasses. "He left quite early. About four o'clock."

"Did he say where he was going?"

"No."

"He didn't give any indication?"

"None at all."

Lefty stopped sipping his beer long enough to add a few words. "Phil got into a row with a couple of lads and that pissed him off."

Conteh quickly picked up on this and asked: "Who were these lads?"

Hanks, having previously been economical with words, was now more forthcoming. "Brothers called Isaac and

Craig Garrett. They gave Phil a mouthful and he left in a huff. He probably went looking for his mates Kerscher and Hopper."

***

Dimbleby and Conteh next visited the Garrett brothers in the flat they shared.

Conteh looked around the brightly painted living room, noting that items of audio equipment made it resemble a recording studio. She couldn't help wondering if they had been obtained by dishonest means.

Both brothers insisted they had not taken their argument with Andrews any further.

"So what was the row about?" asked Dimbleby.

"Bloody referendums," snapped Issac, the taller, scruffier of the two. "Phil said Scotland would refuse to stay in the UK if they were given another vote. He got the needle when I told him that I'd never known Scottish women to say 'no'."

"Yeah," added Craig, stroking his goatee in the manner of a wise man, which he clearly was not. "The silly bastard couldn't take a joke. He accused us of insulting 'his women folk'. I told him he needn't worry about women - he was a boring old fart who only got it out of his trousers to have a piss behind the bushes."

"Charming!" said Conteh, unable to suppress a slight smile.

"Sorry, love. But Andrews was asking for it. He swore at us and became really lippy. I told him to keep his mouth shut if he knew what was good for him."

"So what happened?"

"Nothing - he left soon afterwards."

"And did you two go after him to sort him out?" asked the policewoman.

"No way," Isaac assured them. "We had better things to do,"

"Such as?"

"Drinking!"

"Did you ever have any drinking sessions with Andrews' mates Denton Kerscher and Keith Hopper?" asked Dimbleby.

"We're not that desperate for friends," joked Isaac. "Kerscher thinks too much of himself and Hopper's a bit of an oddball. He once told a few of us in the pub he'd be happy to give us some vegetables from his allotment, but when Craig and I went round to ask him for some he told us to sod off."

Dimbleby shook his head. "Perhaps you two have the knack of rubbing people up the wrong way."

***

The last ports of call for Conteh and Dimbleby were the homes of Kerscher and Hopper.

Conteh observed that Kerscher's latest flat was much

tidier than she expected following her last visit to him on the day after Holly Claskey's murder.

But she focused her thoughts fully on what the man had to say in answer to Dimbleby, who immediately cut to the chase. He said: "Your friend Phil Andrews has gone missing. When is the last time you saw him?"

Kerscher recalled: "We were in the Golden Swan until closing time on Saturday and then went our separate ways."

"Did you arrange to see Mr Andrews again the next day?" asked Dimbleby.

"We just left it that we might have a drink on Sunday afternoon or evening, depending when we were free. The Gnome - sorry Keith Hopper - has an allotment off Gorringe Road and told us he was going there on Sunday to do some work on it. I was at home watching football on TV. I did go to the Golden Swan around teatime, but Phil had already left and Keith didn't turn up."

Conteh followed up: "Did you speak to Mr Andrews on the phone after you saw him on Saturday night?"

"No. I rang his mobile but he didn't answer."

"His mobile? We haven't located one in his name."

"It was my old Samsung. I only gave it to him last week."

***

Conteh reflected that Kerscher's flat had been like a palace compared with Hopper's dilapidated cottage in which a variety of items were left scattered about. And on a coffee table was an ashtray crying out to be emptied.

She and Dimbleby declined the offer to sit on a battered old sofa.

Hopper was also emphatic that he had not seen or heard from Andrews since Saturday night.

"I've no idea where he might be. Perhaps he's left Mary and gone off with a fancy woman." The Gnome laughed at his own feeble joke, and then drew on his cigarette.

"Did he ever say anything to make you feel he and Mary were having marriage problems?" asked Conteh.

"He moaned about her at times but they seemed happy enough. Mary loved cooking for him and I'd give her vegetables from my allotment. If you'd like some fresh fruit and veg, dear, just let me know."

Hopper drew more deeply on his cigarette, causing him to cough and splutter.

"Those things will kill you," Conteh told him, glancing at an empty packet of Rothmans Kingsize on the floor.

"Nah. There's more chance of me dying in a road accident," Hopper scoffed, treating the police officers to a grin that exposed the gap where his missing front tooth had once been.

"Or perhaps at the hands of a killer," Dimbleby told him. "Especially as you're a friend of Denton Kerscher."

"What's that supposed to mean?" asked Hopper, bending the filter on his king size and stubbing it out in the over-full ashtray.

Dimbleby smirked and explained his taunt: "Well, some people close to Denton either get killed or go missing, don't they?"

CHAPTER FORTY-THREE

Thursday, March 28th, 2020

Livermore decided to have a brainstorming session with his team, most of whom felt that Holly Clancey had been killed by Denton Kerscher - but there were several 'votes' for Kyle Carter and some for Fabio Camaggio, who had conveniently taken a trip to Italy.

"Let me throw another name into the hat," said Livermore, looking at each team member in turn. "Could our killer be the missing Philip Andrews? Either something unpleasant has happened to him or he has done a runner. And, if so, why?"

Conteh provided an answer. "I don't think he's the killer Gov. It was his 25th wedding anniversary on the day Miss Clancey was killed and he took his wife to a rare meal out that night. The restaurant manager confirms it."

O'Sullivan quipped: "Twenty-five years of marriage - what a milestone. Did he splash out and treat his wife to lobster and champagne at The Grand Hotel?"

"No. He opted for a mixed grill and house wine at The Harvester." Conteh's reply brought a few ripples of laughter. "The Harvester staff remember Andrews because they got his order wrong and had to apologise to him for taking so long to bring the correct dish. I've had another word with his wife and she confirms they did not get home until almost 10pm. When she went to bed he was watching TV as usual."

Livermore rubbed his bristly chin thoughtfully. "He could have nipped out to the pub and come across Miss Clancey when her car broke down."

Dimbleby agreed. "That's quite possible, Gov. and Andrews would have walked along the road in which she broke down on his way to the pub. But if he was the killer, it would be rather odd for him to then carry on life as normal before going missing."

Livermore nodded. "Good point, Chris. But we have all seen cases where guilt has driven killers to do strange things."

CHAPTER FORTY-FOUR

Thursday, March 28th, 2019

After discovering that Camaggio had returned from Italy, Dimbleby made a return visit to his office, this time with Conteh.

Once again the fashion house boss indignantly protested his innocence and insisted that Holly Clancey was just an employee he hardly knew.

"Is that right?" said Dimbleby. "Then perhaps you could explain this picture of the two of you together."

He took the picture out of an envelope he had been holding and laid it on Camaggio's desk.

The overweight, ageing lothario's bushy eyebrows shot up in an expression of shock. But he quickly regained his composure.

"That picture means nothing. I often have photos taken with employees. I think this one was at an exhibition - I didn't even remember it."

The unfashionably dressed Dimbleby was determined to hold his own against the immaculately and expensively attired businessman.

"Are you expecting me to believe that you do not recall going on a date with one of your employees who was subsequently murdered?

"It was hardly a date," scoffed the Italian. "She came with me to the exhibition at the Towner to represent our company."

Dimbleby opted to out-bluff a bluffer. "And was she representing your company when you made advances to her afterwards?"

"How dare you suggest such a thing!" stormed Camaggio, his cheeks reddening. "That's an absolute lie."

"It's time for you to come clean, Camaggio. This is a murder investigation so stop messing us about."

"You've no right to make such a wild accusation. I will be complaining to your superiors."

Conteh calmly stepped in. "We are focused on finding a murderer and will take all necessary steps to do so. If you can't help us, we will probably ask the Press to reprint this picture of you with Holly. Perhaps their readers might be able to provide further information."

Dimbleby added: "And maybe we should have another word with members of your staff."

Camaggio ran a large hand through his thinning silver hair as he appeared to be considering the possible implications.

"Alright," he said at length. "I did try my luck with Holly but she wasn't having any of it. We never had a sexual relationship."

"Did you visit her at her apartment?" asked Conteh.

"Yes, just the once. That was long before she was murdered. Her death was a complete shock to me."

"So can you remember where you were on the night she was killed?" Dimbleby wanted to know.

"Yes, I was shagging my secretary. She'll confirm it. Does that satisfy you?"

***

Nottage and DC Valerie Jones found Kyle Carter's former girlfriend Hazel Tweedy to be a sad case.

She had an attractive elfin cropped hair style, but her cheeks were sunken and she looked painfully thin.

After ushering the two officers into her poorly furnished lounge, she told them how her volatile relationship with Carter had left her suffering from depression.

Nottage felt sorry for the dowdy young woman as she continued: "Kyle was fine when we first got together, but then he'd be a real bastard at times."

"In what way?" asked DC Jones.

"He was always wanting sex and didn't appreciate that sometimes I'd be tired after going out to work as a cleaner. If I didn't perform to his satisfaction he'd call me a worthless slut or other such names."

"And what would happen if you refused?" asked Nottage, making eye contact with the woman.

"He'd hit me. Once I told him I'd go to the police but he said it would be my word against his."

"Presumably you had cuts or bruises," Jones prompted.

"There would have been medical evidence to back you up. I believe you went to hospital for treatment on one occasion."

Hazel's oval, freckled face expressed concern. "It wasn't that easy. Kyle said he'd tell the police I'd hit him first. And he could be very convincing."

"So what happened?" Nottage inquired.

"We had a series of rows and one day he just decided to go. But that wasn't the end of it. For months after he left he would send me insulting emails and texts. Eventually, they stopped - presumably he got fed up or targeted someone else. What's he been up to now?"

Nottage told her: "We're investigating the murder of a young woman who had modelled for a camera club Mr Carter belonged to. He may be able to help us with our inquiries. The dead woman's name is Holly Clancey. Did you know her or hear him speak of her?"

"No, but I haven't seen Kyle for over a year now."

Nottage wondered if Hazel could provide some more useful information about Carter's behaviour. "Can you tell us anything else about these assaults you say he made on you? Were they ever in a calculated manner or always in a fit of temper?"

Hazel bowed her head and murmured: "They were only when he lost his rag with me."

Nottage nodded sympathetically. "And was that usually after you refused to have sex with him?"

The woman began to sob. "Yes. He'd hit me once or twice and shout abuse. But he gave me a real beating after I told him I didn't fancy him anymore."

Nottage went away pondering whether Kyle Carter's rages could make him a killer.

CHAPTER FORTY-FIVE

Thursday, March 28th, 2019

O'Sullivan, having been briefed by his colleagues, knew where he was likely to find the Garrett brothers - and, sure enough, they were drinking in the public bar of the Golden Swan.

After introducing himself and PC Brian Hudson, the blunt officer wasted no time with pleasantries. O'Sullivan told them: "You lads have some explaining to do."

"How's that?" asked Isaac.

"You claimed you did not continue your row with Phil Andrews after he left the pub. But we now have reason to believe you did - and that you took his mobile phone."

"No way," said Craig, spilling some of his drink on his goatee.

"Don't waste my time," O'Sullivan snapped, glaring at the older brother. "When we carried out a trace on his mobile we found that calls had been made from it within 250 square metres of your flat."

The two brothers exchanged furtive glances.

"So what happened?" asked Hudson in a less aggressive manner.

It was Isaac who answered. "OK. We did follow Phil outside and had another 'go' at him. He lost his rag and tried to punch me, but I knocked his arm away and told him to get lost."

"That's right," said Craig. "He swore at us and stormed off. We then saw he'd dropped his mobile so we took it and made a few calls on it."

"Including one to Australia," O'Sullivan pointed out.

"Yeah, we've got a mate there. But we only borrowed the ruddy phone - we didn't steal it. We were just having a laugh."

O'Sullivan would have none of it. "We'll see how funny you find this when you're charged with theft and interfering with a police investigation by lying to us."

"Come off it!" Isaac said defiantly.

Hudson took the trouble to explain. "You two were the last people to see Mr Andrews before he went missing. Did you notice where he went when he left you?"

"No," Craig replied, wiping his still wet goatee. "Phil marched off down the road that way." He pointed to the left. "The old fool was perfectly OK when he left us - we never hit him. And we didn't steal his phone - he dropped it."

Isaac delved into his grubby coat pocket and pulled out a mobile. "Here - take the bloody thing."

CHAPTER FORTY-SIX

Friday, March 29th, 2019

Nottage and Dimbleby managed to track down Bobby Brown to a hotel in Worthing where he was staying while performing at the local theatre.

They chatted in the hotel's poky lounge where the comedian had been enjoying a beer.

Nottage tried not to show his disapproval when the man cockily insisted that his fling with Pippa Mercer had been a "one-nighter".

"Why didn't you see her again?" he asked.

"She wasn't really my type, mate."

"I thought you fancied her."

"Yeah, but she wasn't up for it so I didn't waste any more time on her," he replied, smirking.

"You mean she didn't prove to be the easy lay you expected?"

"Something like that."

Dimbleby, who until now had been the 'silent partner', seized the opportunity to ask: "Did that piss you off, Mr Brown? Perhaps you got so annoyed you attacked her."

"You couldn't be more wrong, mate."

Nottage challenged: "If that's so, you shouldn't have any trouble telling us where you were on May 5th, 2017 when Pippa Mercer was murdered?"

He was confident the man would not be able to remember.

But Brown fished in his pocket for his iPhone. "What date did you say?" he asked, searching for information in his calendar app.

"May 5th, 2017. Can you prove where you were on that date?"

"As a matter of fact I can, mate. I was in the middle of the English Channel doing my act on a cruise ship."

He looked at his phone for further details. "It was a five-day booking and on May 5th we were anchored in northern France."

***

On the drive back to HQ, with Dimbleby at the wheel, Nottage took a call from his wife on his mobile.

"What's up, love?" he asked.

"Having our daughter at home all week is driving me mad," she said.

Nottage's mind was elsewhere and he couldn't really get his head round Kim's problem. "I thought Niki had been studying hard during her suspension. That's what she told me last night."

He could hear his wife snigger at the other end of the phone. "I hope you're better at sussing out criminals than you are your daughter, Jeff. Niki's simply been going through the motions. She's spent this morning in bed and when I try to talk to her she either ignores me or answers with a grunt.

"I've just lost my temper with her. Her response was to roll her eyes and mutter something inaudible under her breath. I need you here to help me deal with this."

Nottage groaned, partly at being made to feel guilty and partly because of Dimbleby's irritatingly slow driving. "Sorry, Kim. I can't leave work early, I'm in the...

"...middle or a murder investigation," she finished for him. "Same old story."

Her husband felt guilty and now focused on the problem. "I think you should try the 'carrot and the stick' routine," he said. "Tell Niki that if she knuckles down we'll buy her the new sneakers she wants, but if she doesn't we'll ground her for a month. That should do the trick."

***

An upbeat Livermore had some good news to share when Nottage checked in with him.

"We've had a possible breakthrough," his boss told him. "Kyle Carter's so-called watertight alibi doesn't stand up. He did clock in at 8.45pm for work at the hospital on the night of the murder and clocked out at 6am as he told us. But we've been going through the hospital's CCTV cameras and, although they confirm him being on site at various times, they also show him appearing to leave the premises just before 10pm. They record him going towards the car park.

"Furthermore, later that night his car was seen on CCTV being driven within a mile of Holly Clancey's apartment. So he knew the victim and can be placed near the murder scene."

Nottage and Livermore exchanged smiles. "It doesn't sound good for Mr Carter, does it, Gov?"

"No it doesn't, Jeff. With any luck he's still banged up awaiting to appear in court for having sex with an underage girl. Let's have another chat with him, shall we?"

The DCI phoned DI Monahan at Eastbourne nick.

"Hello, Lucinda," he said brightly. "We want to interview Mr Carter again. Do you still have him under lock and key?"

"Unfortunately, not," she responded. "He's no longer in custody. He came up in court this morning charged with indecent assault and was given bail."

"Bugger," Livermore muttered under his breath.

"Sorry?"

"I said BUGGER."

CHAPTER FORTY-SEVEN

Saturday, March 30th, 2019

Livermore and his wife both received letters from Eastbourne Hospital on Saturday morning which they opened while eating breakfast.

He tried to take in the contents of his message from Dr Morgan in Respiratory Medicine but was distracted by Evelyne reading hers aloud TWICE.

"Did you listen to what I just read to you, Harvey?" she demanded, brandishing her letter in front of him. "I've been given an appointment to treat my stress and I'd like you to come with me. I'm still spaced out by that lunatic vandalising our home and my car. I need your support - it's time you put me before that bloody job of yours."

"Of course, luv."

He at last managed to read Dr Morgan's missive, giving him the telephone number of a surgeon's secretary at Guy's Hospital to make an initial appointment regarding an operation for the removal of the objects in his right lung which might be cancerous.

As Livermore considered the matter, he reached across for a slice of toast, but his wife smacked his hand.

"No!" she said firmly. "That toast is for me, Harvey. You shouldn't eat too much bread with your stomach problems or you'll be stuck on the loo."

'Bloody hell!' he thought. 'Goodness knows what Evelyne would be like if I told her I might have cancer.'

Livermore left the toast and stuffed the letter into his pocket. He would wait six months to have another scan - and hope that if he had cancer it didn't spread.

***

Grace Conteh had a rare weekend off and intended to enjoy some quality time with 'the girls'.

But after spending an extra couple of hours in bed on Saturday morning, she wasted almost as long making fruitless telephone calls to friends who told her they already had plans for the rest of the weekend.

By the time she'd washed and dried her black curly hair it was well past mid-day.

She lifted her spirits by cooking one of the dishes her mother served back in Senegal. There was sufficient chicken in the fridge to make stew and soon it was simmering in peanut butter sauce together with yams, potatoes and carrots.

Grace ate her meal with a glass of wine and tried to relax by playing music. But she couldn't stop thinking of Barbie Dickinson having her latest complaint ignored.

The PC found it hard to accept that the woman would be so stupid as to make up a story about a voyeur after being caught out falsely accusing Kerscher of assaulting her.

Grace had once been the victim of a sex pest herself and knew how upsetting it was.

On an impulse, Grace decided to pay the dizzy blonde a visit, and was relieved to find her in.

She told Barbie she'd come to follow up on her complaint and was grudgingly invited into the woman's untidy lounge.

"I can only spare you ten minutes because I'm going out with a girlfriend," Grace was informed.

"OK, Barbie, let's cut to the chase. Are you sure the bloke you saw was a voyeur?"

"A what?"

"A Peeping Tom."

"Yes, I bloody well am. He was staring through the gap in the curtains in my bedroom window and having a good eyeful."

Grace, remembering O'Sullivan's scornful remarks, smiled weakly to hide any scepticism. "I understand you were getting dressed rather than undressed."

"That's right. I'd just come out of the shower. The bastard must have been watching me putting on my underwear before I realised he was there."

After pausing for breath, she continued: "Bloody hell, he would have also seen me checking my breasts in the mirror."

"Can you describe him?"

"Not really. He looked so shocked to be spotted that he almost choked. The pig spat out a fag and ran off."

"What sort of features did he have?"

"It was all so quick that I didn't get a proper look at him."

Grace took a sharp intake of breath, which prompted Barbie to exclaim: "I'm not making this up, yer know."

"Why should we believe you this time, Barbie? That story you invented about Denton Kerscher not only wasted police time, it could have got an innocent man convicted of assaulting you."

Barbie broke off eye contact and looked down at her lounge floor, apparently in shame. "Yeah, I'm sorry I did it. But Kerscher wasn't some wide-eyed innocent, was he? I only picked on him because he'd already assaulted his girlfriend."

Grace put her thoughts into words: "How did you know that?"

"It was in the papers, wasn't it? Didn't they say he'd also killed his previous girlfriend?"

"No," Grace corrected. "He was found not guilty of murdering her."

"Well, there's no smoke without fire," Barbie persisted. "When I saw his name on the parcel that I took in for him, I knew exactly who he was and what he'd done. The name 'Denton Kerscher' isn't one you're likely to forget, is it?

"And when he came to collect his parcel, I had a nasty feeling about him. He might not have touched me but he made me feel uncomfortable the way he stared at my tits. I invented the story about him groping me to try to get my boyfriend back. It didn't work and my boyfriend and I have both moved on, so I've no reason to lie this time."

The policewoman was finally convinced. After assuring Barbie she would do all she could, Grace went outside the bedroom window to check for possible footprints. The ground was hard so there weren't any prints, but she found evidence of a different kind.

CHAPTER FORTY-EIGHT

Saturday, March 30th, 2019

Nottage had made two visits to Kyle Carter's flat, only to find he was out both times.

The peeved policeman talked to neighbours, who told him they'd not seen Carter for two days. Further inquiries revealed that he hadn't turned up for work at the hospital.

Nottage obtained a search warrant and went with Dimbleby to gain access to the suspect's top floor, sparsely furnished abode.

The bulb had blown in the main living room light, so they had to rely on a small lamp and a torch.

"This is a real dump," said a disgusted Nottage. "And it smells, too."

Dimbleby began flicking through a large pile of newspapers and magazines stacked against a wall. "Not surprisingly, these mags are full of porn."

"What about the newspapers?" asked Nottage. "Perhaps Carter was keeping particular news items. How far do those papers go back, Chris? Do any of them cover Holly Clancey's murder?"

His colleague examined the tabloids more carefully and eventually replied: "Yes. These two have stories about her. And there may be more. I'll keep checking."

Nottage, who was going through the draws of a battered old desk, cursed when dust blurred the lenses of his glasses. But after using his shirt to clean them, he also made a significant find.

"Look at these!" he said, opening a folder full of negatives and pictures. "They're of a model either in a state of undress or completely nude. There's loads of them. And, guess what, they're all of Holly Clancey."

CHAPTER FORTY-NINE

Sunday, March 31st, 2019

Grace managed to get up earlier on Sunday. She donned a sports top and shorts to do a vigorous workout, involving squats, jumps and lunges that stretched her long, shapely legs until they glistened with sweat.

The young policewoman decided to visit a car boot sale in Pevensey but was held up by a friend telephoning to apologise for not being able to meet her the previous day.

Arriving at the sale at 11.30am, Grace was surprised - and disappointed - to see several stallholders already starting to pack up.

"I thought this was supposed to last until one o'clock," she moaned to a woman putting away some of the plates, dishes, cups and other crockery on her table.

"It all depends on the weather and how many people come along," the woman told her.

"I see," said Grace, looking up at the cloudy sky. "I'd better get a move on before everyone leaves." As she spoke two stallholders finished packing up and got in their cars.

Grace quickly checked the stalls and tables that were still open. She focused on three next to each other, one run by a middle-aged English couple, containing gardening equipment and plants, the second offering clothing that was temporarily unattended and the third manned by an elderly Asian man selling virtually everything else.

Grace browsed through his goods, and purchased a book for a pound that she probably wouldn't have time to read.

She spotted several box-loads of DVDs and CDs and asked the man: "Do you have any CDs containing stories rather than music? Audio books, I mean."

"I do but I've not got any romance."

"What about thrillers?" she asked.

"I've got an adventure story," he replied, lifting a box of DVDs.

"No, I wanted CDs to play in my car."

"I heard what you said lady and I do have a CD."

The little man eventually found it. "The cover is slightly torn but all the five discs are here and you can have it for a couple of quid," he told her.

Grace felt obliged to buy it, especially as the fantasy adventure story might appeal to her.

"How have you done today?" she asked.

"Not bad."

She picked up and peered at an attractive box.

"That's where I keep my pens," he told her. "It used to contain a large cigarette lighter which I sold to a bloke who didn't want the box. He's a good customer."

"Heavy smoker, is he?" she inquired.

"Yes, he comes into my shop for his cigarettes. He stocked up with 600 Benson and Hedges the other week."

"Nice one," she said. "Are those filter-tip?"

"You're not a smoker, are you lady? Yeah, they're filter-tip. Anything else you'd like to know?"

Yes," she said, taking out her warrant card and flashing it at him. "What does he look like?"

CHAPTER FIFTY

Sunday, March 31st, 2019

Conteh phoned the office and was disappointed to find that 'Mr Grumpy' Mike O'Sullivan was the most senior officer on duty, but she told him her theory.

"Let's get this right," said Mike. "You believe that Philip Andrews might have been the peeper who Barbie says was outside her bedroom window. And he was so worried at being seen by her that he either went into hiding or topped himself."

"That's what I've just been telling you."

"But this is just a hunch, isn't it, Grace? You're simply assuming that because you found a discarded half-smoked Benson and Hedges King Size outside Barbie's window, and you think Andrews smokes that brand, it's likely to be his. That's a bit flimsy, isn't it?"

Grace was becoming exasperated. "There's more to it than that," she insisted. "Denton Kerscher must have had plenty to say about Barbie so his pal Andrews would have been aware of what a looker she was."

O'Sullivan was far from convinced. "If that's the case it could equally apply to Kerscher's other mate Keith Hopper."

"No. Hopper smokes Rothmans. I saw an empty packet

on the floor when Chris and I interviewed him at his cottage."

"And what makes you so sure the king size brand Andrews smokes is Benson and Hedges?"

"One of the stall holders at the local car boot sale supplies Benson and Hedges King Size filter tipped to a man called Pete whose description fits that of Andrews."

"OK. But Andrews must be one of countless thousands who smoke that brand of Benson and Hedges. It proves nothing, does it?"

"Well, it's worth looking into, isn't it?"

O'Sullivan was not won over. "Let's wait until the fag you found has been checked for fingerprints or DNA. Then it will be up to someone from CID to investigate, not us. Our job is to track down a killer, not bother with some pathetic little creep who gets his kicks looking at women in their undies."

Grace was seething. "Sod you, Mike."

"You're clearly not aware of the latest developments that have taken place while you've been off duty, Grace. We now have a main suspect for the murder of Holly Clancey in Kyle Carter.

"He's the guy who you told us sent Holly cheeky Facebook messages. He also took loads of nude pictures of her at a camera club where she was a model. Carter's been caught out by CCTV cameras. On the night of the murder they show him sneaking out of Eastbourne Hospital during his shift as a porter, and later that night his car was seen not far from Holly's apartment."

"I didn't know," admitted a surprised Grace. "It sounds like there's a pretty strong case against Carter, but it's not conclusive, is it?"

"You take a lot of convincing, don't you Grace? Well, the clincher is that a pair of shoes in Carter's bedroom appear to match footprints in the hall leading to Holly's apartment. They're the same size and the soles have the same pattern. We're just waiting for forensics to confirm they're a perfect match."

"Has Carter admitted anything?"

"He seems to have done a runner. We've got everyone out looking for him. So a possible voyeur is not very high on our list of priorities. I was due to go off duty 20 minutes ago and I'm not hanging around much longer. I've got a lady friend waiting for the pleasure of my company."

"Really Mike? She must be unique - I can't think of any women I know who would find that a pleasure."

"Very funny. Unfortunately, I have no more time to waste listening to you droning on like a jabbering parrot, Grace. I suggest we leave your concerns until tomorrow. OK?" The phone went dead.

CHAPTER FIFTY-ONE

Monday, April 1st, 2019

Livermore was furious when he saw Gerald Truelove's front page story with the headline 'POLICE LET MURDER SUSPECT GO'.

Truelove claimed Livermore and his team were urgently looking for Kyle Carter in connection with the murder of Holly Clancey.

His story revealed that Carter had been in custody up to three days ago after being charged with indecently assaulting an underage girl. But he had been released on bail.

The DCI almost choked as he read the paragraph: "It begs the question: why did the police let a murder suspect go?"

His temper got the better of him. He screwed up the paper before hurling it towards the waste bin. As usual, his aim was poor and it ended on the floor.

Livermore swore, shook his head and called in Nottage.

"Have you seen Gerald Truelove's story this morning, Jeff?"

"Yes, Gov. He's making us look right idiots, isn't he?"

Livermore ignored the question and asked one of his own. "Do you think anyone in our team is leaking information to him? I'm beginning to wonder if he's that good at uncovering facts - or if someone's feeding them to him. I'd hate to think some silly sod has been talking to him."

"No, Gov - certainly not one of our regulars. But we've had so many people seconded to the team, one of them might have spoken out of turn. I'll remind them all that if anyone leaks anything there will be serious consequences - they could be instantly suspended, charged and convicted for interfering with the course of justice.

"But I reckon it's more likely to be one of the people we've interviewed who may have spoken to the Press. I'll do my utmost to find out."

Livermore nodded. "Good. I'll leave it for you to deal with, then. Meanwhile, let's trace Kyle Carter before these Press stories terrify every woman in East Sussex."

CHAPTER FIFTY-TWO

Monday, April 1st, 2019

Chris Dimbleby regarded himself as a cautious driver and he hated car chases. Now he feared he could be involved in one.

Extensive inquiries revealed that Carter had borrowed his brother's red Vauxhall Astra, and Automatic Number Plate Recognition cameras spotted it being driven along Eastbourne sea front shortly after 5pm.

Dimbleby, driving an unmarked Volvo V40, accompanied by DC Valerie Jones, was in the nearest police car and sped to the location.

His disregard for the speed limit took them within sight of the Astra.

"Bloody hell!" he exclaimed. "Carter's making for Beachy Head."

"Do you think he's planning to top himself?" asked Jones.

"Who knows? Radio for backup."

She quickly did so.

When the red car approached one of the UK's most notorious suicide spots it veered off the road.

Dimbleby gave chase across a long stretch of rough grassland leading to the chalk cliffs, which rose up to 530ft out of the sea.

It was a bone-shuddering ride for the two officers as their high-performance Volvo tore over dips in the ground at almost 100mph.

Just 50 yards from the cliff edge, they out-sped the Astra and began to cut in front of it, causing the two cars to collide.

The vehicles went into a skid on the wet grass before locking together and coming to a juddering halt.

"Are you alright?" a shocked Dimbleby yelled at Jones, whose normal tight-lips had shot open in alarm.

"Yes," she shouted back. "Let's see if he is."

Carter provided the answer by revving the Astra but one wheel was in a pothole and he was unable to dislodge it. He promptly jumped out and ran towards the cliff edge.

"Stop!" Dimbleby cried out, chasing after him. "Let's talk this through."

The frantic man stopped and replied: "There's nothing to talk about. You know what I did to her. I'm going to end it all."

The two men stood, panting, staring at each other for a few seconds. Dimbleby moved slowly forward and said: "Let us help you."

But Carter turned and ran the last few yards to the cliff edge as Jones, having joined the pursuit, pleaded: "Don't - please don't."

A breathless Dimbleby got within touching distance of Carter and made a grab at his ponytail. But he could not prevent the man hurling himself off the cliff.

Dimbleby was left with a tuft of hair in his hand and looked on in horror as Carter plunged through the air before landing on the rocks below.

CHAPTER FIFTY-THREE

Tuesday, April 2nd, 2019

The next morning Livermore held another meeting of his team minus Dimbleby and Jones.

The DCI created a solemn mood as he spoke in a sombre tone while recapping the details of Kyle Carter's suicide.

"Despite the heroic efforts of DS Dimbleby and DC Jones to stop him, Carter threw himself off the top of Beachy Head. Chris and Valerie are now being treated for the trauma they suffered. But they have given full accounts of what happened and reported that seconds before Carter jumped he said: 'You know what I did to her'."

There were several mutterings and O'Sullivan claimed: "That's as good as admitting he killed Holly Clancey."

Livermore nodded. "It would certainly appear to be."

Conteh spoke up from the middle of the room. "Sorry, Gov, but we can't be certain he was referring to Holly, can we? He may have been talking about the underage girl he was caught having sex with in the back of his car."

Livermore respected her opinion. "That's a good point, Grace. But it's far more likely he would commit suicide over a murder than having his way with a 15-year-old.

"The evidence we've got points to him being obsessed

with Holly Clancey and killing her. Forensic tests have confirmed his footprints were among those in the hall outside her apartment. They're a perfect match. And a neighbour has identified him as being the man she saw loitering around outside Holly's block on the night of the murder."

Nottage confirmed: "That's right. One of the PCs making house to house inquiries was told by a neighbour called Kitty Brooks that a man answering Carter's description was outside Miss Clancey's block on the night of the murder.

"Miss Brooks has since been shown a picture of Carter and is certain it was him because while she was parking her car that night she almost backed into him. She says he was hanging around looking shifty and when someone came out of the apartment block he went in while the door was still open."

"But why did he switch from stalker to killer?" asked Conteh.

Livermore attempted to provide the answer. "Perhaps he wormed his way into her apartment and was thinking all his fantasies about her were going to come true. Instead, Holly rejected him and he flipped."

He turned to Nottage. "Perhaps you could go over what you discovered in his flat, Jeff."

"Certainly, Gov. After Holly modelled at his camera club, Carter kept over 40 pictures he'd taken of her. They were all of her in the nude or in various states of undress.

190

One of the pictures had smudges of semen on it where he must have masturbated. This shows exactly what he meant in a saucy Facebook message he'd sent Holly, saying he'd got some great pictures of her and would like to give her one."

O'Sullivan joined in the discussion. "But there's no evidence to suggest Carter killed Pippa Mercer as well."

"No," said Livermore. "Nothing connects Carter with Pippa's murder."

This was the cue for O'Sullivan to return to his old theme. "So it still looks as though Denton Kerscher killed Pippa and the bastard got away with it."

Livermore wondered if this stubborn DS was incapable of seeing some things with an open mind. But he confined himself to saying: "The fact remains Kerscher was found not guilty. Our task now is to focus on the other suspects."

"How are Dimbleby and Jones?" asked Conteh.

"They're still in shock. Seeing Carter throw himself to his death was obviously an horrific experience. But they've both said they want to return to work as soon as possible."

O'Sullivan remarked: "What I can't get my head round is old Chris driving like a bat out of hell in a car chase. I've never known him to go over 30 before."

Nottage replied with similar black humour. "It must have been hair-raising, but that's a sensation you can no longer experience, Mike."

This wisecrack brought bursts of laughter and even the balding O'Sullivan had the grace to smile.

***

Livermore arranged for the Press Office to put out a statement saying that, following Kyle Carter's death, police were not currently investigating anyone else regarding the murder of Holly Clancey.

This prompted dramatic headlines including 'MURDER SUSPECT COMMITS SUICIDE' and 'SUSPECTED KILLER TAKES OWN LIFE'.

Some papers quoted 'a source' as saying that Carter had taken nude pictures of Miss Clancey and then stalked her. The media concluded that he threw himself off Beachy Head before police could charge him with Miss Clancey's murder.

CHAPTER FIFTY-FOUR

Tuesday, April 2nd, 2019

Conteh took the opportunity to tell Nottage and Livermore about her suspicions regarding Phil Andrews being a possible voyeur.

Livermore seemed very interested but told her: "We'd only be able to prove it's him if the half-smoked cigarette you found outside Barbie Dickinson's bedroom window has Andrews' DNA on it.

"Unfortunately, during the time it was lying on the ground there was heavy rainfall so it's unlikely forensics will find anything."

Nottage asked: "Did Miss Dickinson get a good look at him?"

"Not really."

"So she can't give us a description."

"No, Gov."

"We haven't got much, have we, Grace?" Nottage summed up. "It could have a bearing on him going missing, but it's just a theory isn't it?"

Livermore reiterated what O'Sullivan had said previously: "A case of voyeurism is something for CID to look into, but without DNA they probably won't be able to do anything."

They were interrupted by the phone ringing. Livermore took the call and, upon hearing his wife's distressed voice, was shocked to learn that about five tonne of wet concrete had been deposited on their driveway.

"Bloody hell!" he snapped. He managed to say some suitably soothing words to Evelyne who blurted out that she'd found the concrete on their drive upon returning from shopping.

After assuring her he would 'sort it' and hanging up, Livermore told Nottage and Conteh what had happened.

"It's obviously the same sick bastard who smashed our windows. This has got to stop!" he snapped.

***

Nottage later reported to his boss that he'd been unable to trace who had arranged for the concrete to be dumped.

"It was ordered from some cowboy firm in Eastbourne," he said. "They were phoned by a man who paid in cash. He put an envelope through their door containing enough money to cover the charges plus a £10 tip."

Livermore cursed under his breath. "What about the call made to them? Can we trace the phone?"

"No luck, Gov. The bastard must have used a burner phone which he obviously discarded. To add insult to injury he not only asked the firm to leave the concrete on your driveway, he placed the order in your name."

Livermore cracked his knuckles so hard it hurt. But he calmly pointed out: "I drew up a list of possible candidates after the paint was thrown over my wife's car - has any progress been made with that?"

"There were 11 names on your list, Gov, and we were able to eliminate eight of them on the basis they had cast iron alibis. Two were out of the country and the other six were banged up in nick."

"So who are the remaining three?"

"Harry Trent, Wayne Briggs and Vinnie Rowlands."

Livermore nodded. "All three are nasty pieces of work and they were furious when my evidence got them put down. Vinnie Rowlands should be easy for anyone to spot - he's a giant who's so ugly they call him 'The Elephant Man'. But I thought he was still inside."

"No. He got out a couple of months ago. Unfortunately, we've come up with no witnesses or CCTV showing that Rowlands, Trent or Briggs were near your wife's car. There's someone else who could be targeting you, of course."

"Who's that?"

"Denton Kerscher."

"He was reporting to the local nick as part of the terms of his bail when my wife's car was covered in paint, Jeff."

"I'm aware of that, Gov. He might not have carried out these acts of vandalism himself but could have paid someone else to do them."

CHAPTER FIFTY-FIVE

Monday, April 8th, 2019

A week later Grace was given the task of checking with anyone who knew the missing Philip Andrews to see if they had heard anything from him. Nobody had!

His wife Mary was desperate for news and Grace was upset that she had none to give the distraught woman.

The young officer got no answer when she called at Keith Hopper's cottage, so went to his allotment where she found him taking a break inside his shed.

"What can I do for you, lovely lady?" asked Hopper when Grace poked her head round the door late that morning.

"Hello, Mr Hopper. I'm Detective Constable Grace Conteh, if you recall. Your friend Phil Andrews is still missing so we're checking to see if anyone has heard anything from him. Have you?"

The scruffily dressed man, wearing a tatty old sweater and dirty corduroy trousers, shook his head. "Nothing!" he said. "Not a word. Look, I'm just brewing some tea - come in and I'll pour you a cup."

Grace's first inclination was to decline the offer, but she changed her mind as she saw Hopper look admiringly at her short brown skirt and matching below-the-knee boots.

'The silly man is so keen to ogle me that he'll probably say far more than he would in a formal interview,' she thought.

"Thanks, Mr Hopper. Plenty of milk and one sugar please." She treated him to a warm smile that made her pleasant features even more appealing.

"Take a seat, luv," he added, unfolding an old wooden chair which he passed to her. "What did you say your name was - Grace is it?"

"Yes."

Both of them sat down and he handed Grace her tea.

"As I mentioned, we're still searching for Phil Andrews. Have you any idea where he might be?"

"Sorry, I can't help you. It's not like old Phil to go off like this."

"Did he have any friends apart from you and Denton?"

"Not really. And when it came down to it we were just drinking pals."

"What about his interests?"

"He wasn't very active, apart from walking and gardening. He liked watching football but he was just an armchair fan."

"Did he ever give you a hand on the allotment?"

"Once or twice, but he wasn't much help. All Phil really wanted when he came here was to have a chat and a cuppa."

"I understand he was a smoker like yourself."

"Yeah, but not in my class. He'd only smoke about 30 a week whereas I go through more than that every day." He pointed to an ashtray full of butts.

Grace saw a packet of Benson and Hedges next to the ashtray. "I thought you smoked Rothmans," she said.

"Yeah, I do normally. But Phil used to buy them cheap for us and the plonker bought me Benson and Hedges by mistake."

The policewoman suddenly realised that it could have been Hopper who spied on Barbie - not Andrews. She put some of her thoughts into words. "We found a half-smoked B&H King Size filter-tip outside the bedroom window of Barbie Dickinson. Did you know her?"

"You mean the tart who accused Denton of touching her up?"

"Yes. Did you go to her flat?"

"And why would I do that?" he asked, glaring.

Grace nervously crossed one leg over the other and noted his change in attitude when her thigh become clearly visible.

"Perhaps Denton told you Barbie was a looker and you decided to check her out. You have an eye for a pretty lady, don't you, Keith?"

She noticed Hopper's expression melt into a smile. He seemed transfixed as the skirt rose an inch.

"I certainly do when the lady is as pretty as you."

"And maybe you wanted to take a look at Barbie?"

Hopper's body language gave him away. His cheeks reddened and he avoided making eye contact.

"You know it was wrong to stare at Barbie, like that,

don't you, Keith?"

"Is looking a crime?"

"Yes, if it's voyeurism and your attentions are unwelcome, Keith."

"But they're not unwelcome with you, are they?" he said, reaching out his grubby right hand and patting her knee. The pat turned into a stroke.

"Please stop that," she scolded, and brushed his hand away.

Grace realised she was in danger of breaching police procedures if she continued without making an arrest. But she thought *'what the hell - no-one is going to know if I take this a bit further.'*

To give herself some thinking time, she sipped her tea, found it wasn't to her liking, and put it down before trying a different tact. "You and Denton are very close, aren't you?"

"Yeah, we go way back. We're good mates."

"Good enough mates for you to cover for him?"

The glare returned as Hopper retorted: "Now what are you suggesting?"

"Perhaps you decided to help out an old mate by giving him an alibi on the night Holly Clancey was murdered. Maybe you said you were talking to him outside the pub for much longer than you actually were."

"Nonsense!" he snapped.

She tried to defuse the situation she had created by smiling at him. "OK, perhaps you simply got the time wrong. After all, Denton admitted he didn't remember how long he was with you."

Hopper's cheeks reddened, his eyes narrowed and he looked to his left.

Grace realised she wouldn't get any further by continuing to antagonise him. She re-crossed her well-toned legs and flashed him another smile. The Gnome grinned back, exposing his missing tooth, and stared into her dark upturned eyes. He replaced his hand on her knee, edged closer and murmured: "You're really something."

Grace suddenly became aware she was getting out of her depth. "Perhaps we should continue this conversation at the station," she said, preparing to get up.

But she stopped when he snapped: "I don't like being teased and then turned down."

The remark jarred with Grace and brought a new thought that hadn't occurred to her - or her colleagues - before.

'If Kerscher and Hopper weren't together so long outside the pub then it meant that Hopper didn't have an alibi either. How will he react if I try a shot in the dark?'

She knew she was about to go much further than she should but couldn't resist.

"What do you mean you don't like being turned down? Is that what happened when you went to Holly Clancey's apartment?"

"Who said I went there?"

Grace's heart started to beat faster. Her guess might pay unexpected dividends. Whatever she said next was vital - it could either make him clam up or open up. She chose her words carefully. "What did Holly say to upset you, Keith?"

"The silly cow invited me in and gave me the 'come on'. But when I suggested we should go into the bedroom she laughed out loud. The bitch actually said: 'Never in a million years'.

"So what did you do, Keith?"

"I lost it."

Grace waited for him to continue, which he eventually did. "Holly stopped smirking when I picked up her ashtray and bashed her on the head with it. The little tart had offered her body to Denton on a plate, but thought it was a joke to have sex with me. Would you find it a joke, Grace?"

The frightened policewoman froze, but when his fingers inched higher she placed her right hand over them to halt their progress.

She tried to remain calm, sliding her other hand into her bag to grasp her mobile and fumbled for the speed dial number to Livermore, but got it hopelessly wrong.

'Shit, I could be in trouble here'.

The Gnome was staring at her so Grace withdrew her hand from the bag and tried to carry on talking normally.

"And what about Denton's previous girlfriend Pippa Mercer? Did she turn you down, too?"

"She was another bitch. She took great delight in teasing me - even letting me touch her on one occasion and then saying 'no'."

"What happened outside her flat, Keith?"

"Pippa had asked me to come round to fix a broken shelf and said she'd make it worth my while. But when I arrived she was on her way out and was actually walking across the road. She'd either completely forgotten inviting me or didn't care that I'd had a wasted journey.

"I walked alongside her and said that if she gave me a chance I'd treat her much better than Denton had. I told her I really fancied her. The cow looked at me as if I was a piece of dirt and asked if I really thought she was that desperate.

"The red mist came over me and I lashed out at her. Pippa made things worse by calling me a nut case and shouting that she'd rather eat her own vomit than have sex with me. So I kicked her until she stopped screaming."

Grace was shocked that this little man she'd dismissed as a pathetic voyeur was actually a violent murderer.

"But if you were so furious with these women why did you take their panties after they'd insulted you?"

"Even though I hated them for ridiculing me, I was gagging for them. But I wasn't stupid enough to hang around. So I took their panties and pleasured myself when I got home."

The Gnome smiled at her, again revealing his missing front tooth.

Grace knew she should arrest him but believed that attempting to do so could put her in danger.

Trying not to show her fear and utter revulsion, the policewoman placed her left hand in her bag again. But before she could reach her mobile he challenged: "What are you doing?"

She removed her hand and said the first thing that came to mind. "I was going to put on some more lipstick. But I can do that later."

This seemed to please him. *'Oh no'*, she thought. *'I've given him the impression I'm encouraging his advances'*.

His grimy fingers were now touching the top of her thigh and she grasped his hand firmly to prevent it progressing further.

"That's enough!" she urged.

"Don't reject me, Grace - I told you I don't like being rejected. I hate prick teasers."

"And I hate people touching me with dirty hands," she shot back bravely.

"I can easily put that right, luv." He got up, went over to the sink and started washing his hands.

Grace was tempted to reach for her mobile again, but Hopper turned round to look at her while reaching for a rather grubby towel.

CHAPTER FIFTY-SIX

Monday April 8th, 2019

Nottage read through the updated reports on his laptop concerning the victimisation of his boss.

Denton Kerscher, Harry Trent and Wayne Briggs had all been able to account for where they were at the time red paint was thrown over Mrs Livermore's car, but Vinnie Rowlands said he was at home alone.

Although nobody actually witnessed the act of vandalism, inquires at local stores revealed that a hooded, tall man had purchased a tin of red paint three days earlier. Unfortunately, he had paid in cash and the shop's CCTV was broken so there was nothing to identify him.

The policeman cursed. *'It all points to The Elephant Man, but I don't have the evidence to arrest him,'* he thought.

Then he had a brainwave. He could use the same 'carrot and stick' routine on Vinnie Rowlands that had worked on his daughter.

'The DI drove to Rowlands' flat and found that the thug was even bigger - and uglier - than he'd imagined.

'Blimey', thought Nottage. *'How the mighty are fallen. This one-time Mr Big's living conditions must be a million times worse than he enjoyed when he resided in a mansion before his downfall'.*

"Well?" demanded Rowlands, "what the bloody hell do you fucking coppers want now?"

Nottage smiled and replied: "We're going to have a nice little chat so invite me in."

"I've fuck all to say to you."

Nottage's smile vanished. "Well fucking listen instead, dickhead, or my next conversation will be with your probation officer who just happens to be on speed dial on my phone. Either we have a chat now or you slam the fucking door - your choice."

Rowlands sighed and let him in. "So what do you bloody want?"

"What I want," replied Nottage, refusing to be intimidated by the giant who was a good four inches taller than him, "is for you to explain yourself. You can start by telling me why you purchased a tin of red paint three days before red paint was thrown over a car belonging to the wife of a policeman?"

"I don't know what you're talking about, mate. I didn't buy any fucking paint."

"Where were you on the morning of Tuesday, March 26th between 9 and 10 am when the car was vandalised?"

"I was here."

"So you're claiming you didn't go out before ten that morning?"

"I didn't say that, did I? I went for a run but that was a lot earlier."

"You take a run early every morning do you?"

"Yeah - so what?"

"Did you take one around 5.30 on the morning of Sunday, March 17th and happen to stop off to smash the windows of an officer's home?"

"I go for my runs at 7am. At 5.30 I was tucked up in bed sound asleep. You've got nothing on me, copper, so why don't you piss off?"

"Don't fuck with me, Rowlands. We won't let this go. If you come up in court for acts of vandalism against a police officer and his wife you could be back in clink for a very long time."

The Elephant Man's imposing figure seemed to shrink and the smirk had been wiped off his face. But he remained defiant. "Are you here to make some sort of deal?"

"Why should I do that?"

"Because while Denton Kerscher and I were banged up in Wormword Scrums we spent two weeks in the hospital ward together."

Nottage hadn't known this and was unable to hide his surprise.

Rowlands became more confident. "You should do your homework, Inspector. Kerscher and I both caught an infection and were in adjoining beds."

"Are you able to give me some new information about him?"

"Maybe."

"OK. Let's hear it. If you tell me what he said to you then it might go in your favour."

"Word on the street is that you reckon Kerscher got away with murdering his first girlfriend and then killed his second. But I'd bet anything that he didn't."

"How's that?"

"He swore to me he didn't kill Pippa whatever her name was."

"So that's that, then. Case closed."

Rowlands shook his head. "You learn to separate fact from bullshit in the nick and this wasn't bullshit. Kerscher kept on about it so much I told him to shut the fuck up. But I believed him. He was almost driving himself mad trying to think who might have done it and once talked about his sex-starved mate who he said fancied Pippa."

"And who was this mate?"

"He called him The Gnome."

"The Gnome - you mean Keith Hopper. Well, it's worth checking out, but this is just speculation. We deal in facts, Rowlands."

"I'm pretty sure Kerscher is no killer - he's not got it in him."

Nottage remained silent, so Rowlands expanded on his theme. "I don't give a shit who goes down for it. But what you stupid bastards seem to have over-looked is that Kerscher isn't the only one who knew both his girlfriends. Hopper did as well and he was probably lusting over them. Look, I'm doing your bloody job for you, mate. So have we got a deal?"

Nottage made eye contact with the thug and told him:

"If you'd read the papers lately you'd have seen that a bloke called Kyle Carter virtually confessed to killing Holly Clancey before he committed suicide. What you've told me is pure supposition so there's no deal to be struck."

But, despite his initial dismissive remark, the copper realised that the time was right to offer a reward combined with a threat of punishment. So he added: "If no further evidence is forthcoming and no more acts of vandalism are committed against DSI Livermore and his wife, we might not charge you."

Rowlands nodded. "I hate that bastard for getting me convicted of murder instead of manslaughter. Any other copper would have accepted there was no intent, but not Livermore. Anyway, perhaps he's suffered enough."

"So you admit it was you?"

"I'm admitting nothing, mate. I'm just saying I know what goes on."

Nottage shook his head. "Enough is enough, Rowlands!"

The giant gave the faintest of nods.

"What about Denton Kerscher? Is he likely to carry on where you've left off by targeting DCI Livermore?"

"Don't make me laugh, mate. He wouldn't have the guts."

"Did Kerscher put you up to doing it for him?"

"I'm not going to say anything to incriminate myself, but I had my own scores to settle with Livermore. I wouldn't be bothered about helping that loser Kerscher."

***

When Nottage got back to his car he phoned Livermore to inform him what Rowlands had revealed.

"Have I got this right, Jeff? You've told Rowlands we're not going to arrest him with smashing my windows, wrecking my wife's car and dumping concrete on my drive?"

Nottage cringed. "I said that if no further evidence comes to light and there are no more acts of vandalism we MIGHT not charge him. Let's face it, Gov, we haven't got enough on him - nobody can positively identify the bastard."

"So he gets off Scot-free. He doesn't even have to pay for the damage he's done."

Nottage chuckled. "Look on the positive side, Gov. Your insurance company will reimburse you - and I believe this has put an end to the vendetta."

He could imagine Livermore cracking his knuckles in frustration as his boss retorted: "And you think I should be grateful?"

"That would be nice, Gov."

When the DCI calmed down he asked: "And what do you make of Rowlands's claims about Keith Hopper?"

"Of course we need to look into them, but, as I told Rowlands, it's pure speculation. Yes, Hopper knew the two victims and might have fancied them, but he had alibis for both murders, didn't he? And Kyle Carter as good as admitted to the second killing."

Nottage gave the matter further consideration and added: "What Kerscher told Rowlands was probably simply said in frustration - he didn't actually accuse Hopper, did he?"

CHAPTER FIFTY-SEVEN

Monday, April 8th, 2019

As Hopper moved towards her, Conteh squirmed in her chair, but told herself not to panic. 'Keep him talking - ask him another question'.

"Is it a relief for you to finally tell someone what you've done, Keith?"

"You're not the first person I've told, sweetheart."

"What do you mean?"

"Phil came round here and caught me finishing myself off over some soft porn magazine. He was shocked, and started lecturing me. I told him women drive men to wank themselves. They love to get us worked up and then refuse us. And that's what got Holly and Pippa killed. They were just prick teasers.

"Phil asked if I had tried it on with them. He realised it was me who killed them and the silly bastard said he was going to tell the police. I couldn't have that, could I?"

Conteh gasped. "What did you do, Keith?"

"I clouted him with my spade until he was dead."

"So where's his body?"

"It's not far away, luv. I dug a big hole in the allotment outside and buried him in it."

Conteh got to her feet, only to be pushed back on to the

chair by Hopper.

At that moment her phone rang and she made a grab for it. Conteh managed to pull the mobile from her bag, but before she could speak into it, Hopper knocked it from her grasp.

As the mobile clattered on the floor, he struck Conteh a ferocious blow to the temple with his fist.

She hit her head on the chair as she fell, and was knocked out cold.

PART THREE

CHAPTER FIFTY-EIGHT

Monday, April 8th, 2019

When Grace came round her head was throbbing with pain. But, even worse, she found to her horror that she had been tied up and gagged - and left lying on the floor of the shed.

She could hear Hopper, somewhere outside, making a noise she couldn't make out at first. Finally, Grace realised he was digging.

'Dear God. Surely he's not going to bury me alive?'

The terrified policewoman tried to strain against the ropes that bound her but only succeeded in grazing her wrists.

After what seemed an eternity she heard footsteps approaching. Hopper came into the shed, panting as he loomed over her. He took only a couple of minutes to regain his breath and then dragged her outside towards a large hole he had dug.

When she was a few feet from it, The Gnome pulled up her skirt and stood staring at her lying at his mercy, with Grace's white panties exposed.

He fiercely ripped them off. Then the disgusting little man gave a sickly smile and put the panties under his nose.

"They smell lovely," he gloated, sniffing the material deeply, before stuffing them in his pocket. "Just a little something for me to remember you by."

Grace glared up at him, her face full of hatred, and saw Hopper's mood suddenly change.

He raged: "You would have turned me down, too, wouldn't you? Bitch, bitch, bitch!"

Her furious attacker twice kicked Grace in the ribs before using his boot to shove the helpless policewoman into the hole.

The Gnome then picked up his spade and started to shovel earth on top of her.

Despite shaking with fear, she frantically tried to loosen the ropes around her wrists, but they would not budge.

The gag prevented Grace shouting out as more earth showered down. She frantically shook her head to prevent the soil going into her eyes and mouth.

Hopper was about to hurl in another shovelful when Grace heard someone shout "Stop that, you bastard."

Although her vision was blurred, she could see the spade snatched away from the hideous little man, who was then knocked flying by a much taller figure. It was Livermore.

Grace blinked repeatedly and could see the policeman jump on top of her tormentor. After a tussle, The Gnome was handcuffed. Then Livermore turned his attentions to Grace, gently wiping the earth off her face before lifting her out of the hole.

When the gag was removed she spluttered: "Thank God, you came, Gov."

CHAPTER FIFTY-NINE

Wednesday, April 10th, 2019

Conteh spent two days in hospital but, immediately upon being discharged, she reported back for duty.

She was given a standing ovation from colleagues before being invited by Livermore to join him and Nottage in his office.

Conteh, whose ribs were still sore from the kicking she had received, was grateful to be given a seat while Nottage stood. But she fiddled nervously with her fingers, anxiously waiting to discover whether her boss would acclaim or condemn her.

His opening remarks kept her guessing. "Well, Grace, I don't know whether to sing your praises or give you a rollicking."

The DCI let his words sink in before continuing: "First I'd like to congratulate you on finding our killer and showing such coolness and bravery."

"Thank you, Gov."

"But you clearly exceeded your brief which was simply to ask if anyone had seen or heard from Phil Andrews."

Conteh had anticipated this and prepared her answer. "When I saw that Hopper's ashtray was full of butts of the same brand of cigarette as that found outside Barbie

Dickinson's bedroom window I felt it was appropriate for me to ask him if he had been there."

"So how did things escalate?" asked Nottage.

"He started to come on to me and put his hand on my leg. When I stopped him going any further he told me he didn't like being teased and then turned down. That remark caused our conversation to switch to the two murdered women and things got out of hand."

Livermore shook his head. "You shouldn't have put yourself in that position, Grace. You almost got yourself killed. It was reckless and a breach of PACE Codes of Practice."

The awkward silence that followed was broken by the popping sound of Livermore cracking his knuckles.

Conteh finally said: "Sorry, Gov. Will action be taken against me?"

She studied the face of her senior officer and was relieved to see the stern look change to a wry smile. "The media are acclaiming you as a heroine, Grace, so I don't think 'Fussy' - sorry, DCS Frampton - will risk a backlash by putting you on a charge for going against police procedures. But you must learn from this and never again turn into a one-woman task force."

"Sorry, Gov. It won't happen again. I tried to speed dial you for backup but I couldn't let Hopper see me do it. I was frightened that if he did so - or I told him he was under arrest - I'd put myself in danger."

Livermore nodded. "I appreciate that, Grace, But you'd

already let things go too far. We need to follow procedures. Going off at half cock could wreck any chance of getting a conviction."

Grace shifted uncomfortably in her chair. She was about to speak but thought better of it and bit her lip.

Livermore continued. "Fortunately, Keith Hopper has made a full confession, but if he'd claimed that you entrapped him then the case against him might have been thrown out. Do you understand?"

"Yes, Gov, you're quite right. Though, with respect, I don't think we would have got him to admit to the murders under normal circumstances."

"Maybe not," conceded the DCI. "But we would have built up a case against him with good old fashioned police evidence."

Grace again decided it was best to keep quiet.

Livermore went on: "For example, a footprint in Holly Clancey's hall is a match for one of Hopper's shoes. It's distinctive because his right foot points slightly inwards. A search of Hopper's cottage has revealed he kept items of women's underwear, which may include the missing panties belonging to the two murdered women. I'm just awaiting a report from forensics."

Nottage added: "We've got a cast iron case anyway. The fact the Governor caught the bastard trying to bury you alive is, of course, the clincher."

Grace turned to Livermore, beaming with appreciation, and told him: "I'm so grateful to you for coming to my rescue, Gov. How did you know I was in trouble?"

"Yeah, what made you go to the allotment?" asked Nottage.

"That was partly due to my own piece of detection - and partly good luck. When you told me Kerscher had said Hopper was sex starved and fancied Pippa Mercer it got me thinking. You dismissed Hopper being our killer, Jeff, because he had alibis for both murders, but it turns out he didn't.

"He had claimed he was with Kerscher when Holly Clancey was attacked, but his mate couldn't remember how long they'd been together. So it was easy for Hopper to tell a lie and give himself a false alibi as well as provide one for Kerscher.

"I quickly looked up the case notes on Pippa Mercer's murder and saw that Hopper's sick grandmother had died before we could ask her to confirm his claim he'd been with her. So alarm bells started ringing, especially as I knew he was among the people Grace was due to question about Phil Andrews. I phoned Grace's mobile and my call was answered almost immediately but she didn't speak..."

"No, Hopper knocked the phone out of my hand," Conteh explained.

Livermore continued: "He stupidly failed to end the call so I heard his attack on you."

Grace smiled at him. "Fortunately, that caused you to come rushing to my rescue. You were my knight in shining armour."

Livermore returned her smile. "But you were so lucky, Grace. There was not enough time for me to get a trace on your mobile so I opted to go to Hopper's allotment. If I'd gone to his cottage first, I'd have been too late to save you."

CHAPTER SIXTY

Wednesday, April 10th, 2019

Livermore was pleased to see that his team members had recovered from recent ordeals and were in good spirits at the next meeting.

"Nice shirt, Chris," O'Sullivan told his old sparring partner. "Get it at Primark, did you?"

"As a matter of fact I did," Dimbleby retorted. "Yours is obviously more expensive, Mike. But it's a bugger when colours run, isn't it?"

The room erupted in laughter and Livermore noted that even O'Sullivan was smiling.

When they got down to business, the DCI explained what had turned Hopper into a killer.

"His medical records indicate mental instability which would cause him to overreact at times. He had deep feelings of abandonment and rejection from an early age.

"His father left the family home when Keith was only six. And the boy didn't appear to get much love from his mother, either. Police records show that she was twice convicted of prostitution. She also admitted child neglect after leaving young Hopper alone at the age of eight while she went out drinking."

Nottage was the first to respond. "That explains why he

couldn't bear rejection."

Dimbleby provided some more light relief by chipping in: "Looking like a garden gnome obviously didn't help him!"

Livermore waited for the laughter to end before speaking again. When he did his facial expression and tone of voice reflected the gravity of the situation. "Sadly, it would appear that both Pippa Mercer and Holly Clancey did the worst thing possible by mocking Hopper. It cost them their lives."

Nottage reflected: "They could never have suspected Hopper would react like that - and neither did we."

O'Sullivan concurred. "No. He came across as a Good Samaritan who gave away produce from his allotment and was willing to do odd jobs for people. He slipped under the radar. And I got it completely wrong about Denton Kerscher. What a bloody idiot I was!"

"You weren't alone in thinking it was Kerscher, Mike," Livermore consoled. "He was the obvious suspect. Kerscher had intense relationships with both the murdered women and assaulted one of them outside a nightclub."

O'Sullivan asked: "Do we now know if Kerscher's drink was spiked at the nightclub as he claimed? Bloody hell, did Hopper do that?"

Livermore grinned because O'Sullivan's seemingly wild theory was probably not far off the mark. "No, Mike, there's no evidence that Hopper was at the nightclub. But Kerscher was given Monkey Dust and guess what we've found at

Hopper's home - Monkey Dust."

"So how did he get it put into Kerscher's drink, Gov?" Nottage wondered.

Livermore's grey eyes lit up. "I can only speculate but, as Kerscher said, there were a lot of people who didn't like him - mainly family members and friends of Pippa Mercer who believed he killed her. Maybe Hopper tipped one of them off that Kerscher was planning to go to the nightclub and gave them some Monkey Dust."

"Blimey!" exclaimed Dimbleby. "If you're right, Gov, that would mean Hopper stitched Kerscher up a second time after letting him go to prison for a crime he didn't commit. Why would he want his drink to be spiked?"

Livermore gave the question some thought. "My guess would be he resented Kerscher poking fun at him. Perhaps he found out that Denton had nick-named him The Gnome. So, although he acted as Denton's friend, he probably disliked the man."

Dimbleby was still puzzled. "But Hopper gave him an alibi for the murder of Holly Clancey," he pointed out.

It was Nottage who answered. "That's where Hopper was clever. By saying Kerscher was with him, Hopper was also giving himself an alibi. I must admit he fooled me."

"What about Carter?" asked Valerie Jones. "Why did he commit suicide when he wasn't the killer?"

A coughing fit prevented Livermore answering, and Conteh suggested: "Perhaps it was simply the fear he would be charged with her murder."

Livermore, having done his homework on the man, was able to give a fuller explanation. "Carter had lots of hang ups. His parents were devout Christian Scientists and he was a disappointment to them. He was always trying to seek their approval without much success because he kept landing himself in trouble. The final straw came when his parents discovered he'd been arrested for having sex with an underage girl. His mother has admitted that she told him they were disowning him.

"Being spurned by the only two people close to him was probably devastating enough. But, as Grace has pointed out, Carter was then horrified to realise he was likely to be charged with the murder of Holly Clancey."

Jones nodded and added: "Did he actually have a relationship with Holly?"

"I doubt it, but he'd become infatuated with her. And after bombarding her with messages on Facebook, Carter began to stalk her. He even hung about outside Holly's home. That's why his shoes matched footprints in the hall leading to her apartment. There's no evidence he actually went inside. Perhaps he lacked the bottle to ring her bell or, if he did, she could have been out."

"Pathetic little sod," remarked Jones.

O'Sullivan was more scathing. "Like Hopper, he was a dangerous sex maniac. Both of them were raving psychos, able to pass themselves off as normal people."

Livermore wasn't convinced. "We'll have to see what the experts say. Our profiler Ralph Vickers did not think the murderer was necessarily a sociopath or psychopath. Hopper was a complex character. He showed few emotions at times, but then revealed jealousy, rage and hatred if he felt rejected."

Conteh had another question. "What's going to happen to Barbie Dickinson, Gov?"

Livermore was touched by Conteh's concern for the naïve girl. "Kerscher says he doesn't wish to give evidence against her. So, after taking into account she was on medication for depression over relationship problems with her boyfriend, she won't be charged with wasting police time. Barbie will get off with a formal caution."

"She's bloody lucky," snapped O'Sullivan.

"Unlike Kerscher," mused Dimbleby. "That poor bastard spent a year in nick for a murder he didn't commit and then got arrested for a second one."

"Yes," said Livermore. "As his Mother said, he wasn't a killer - he was a victim."

***

Kerscher spent that evening walking along a deserted beach in Pevensey.

He eventually stopped and stood for ages looking out to sea, trying to get his head round everything that had happened.

Gazing at the vast expanse of water had a calming effect, yet it was hard to accept that his nightmare had finally ended. He'd accused the police of stitching him up, but he now realised the blame lay with his 'best mate' for letting him take the rap for two murders - that was the real stitch up.

ABOUT THE AUTHOR

Tony Flood was formerly Controller of Information at Sky Television, but spent most of his working life as a journalist on various national and regional papers.

He retired as a journalist when he left national Sunday newspaper The People in 2010 and became an author.

His first book was fantasy adventure SECRET POTION, which went to No. 1 in its category of Amazon bestsellers and has been recommended by other authors for Harry Potter fans.

Tony's celebrity book MY LIFE WITH THE STARS - SIZZLING SECRETS SPILLED! is full of anecdotes and revelations about showbiz and sports personalities, including Eric Morecambe, Elvis Presley, Kylie Minogue, George Best, Frank Sinatra, Joan Collins, Strictly Come Dancing stars, Muhammad Ali and Bobby Moore, with whom he worked.

The versatile Mr Flood then turned to writing in another genre with spicy crime thriller TRIPLE TEASE, endorsed by bestselling writer Peter James, actor Brian Capron and the The Sun newspaper's Stuart Pink.

Tony encourages other writers as president of Anderida Writers of Eastbourne. He also plays veterans football and writes theatre reviews for the Brighton Argus and Eastbourne Herald.

Printed in Great Britain
by Amazon

44305907R00139